Of
Bitter Herbs
and
Sweet Confections

SUSAN SHALEV

Of Bitter Herbs and Sweet Confections

SUSAN SHALEV

ISBN 10: 1729756050
ISBN 13: 978-1729756058

Design:
Studio Maytal Amir

In Memory of Tamar and Avraham Shalev

Chapter 1

Tajikistan, 1945

The State University of Leningrad? How could this be possible? I stare at the school principal with disbelieving eyes. This was not something I had even dared to dream of in my wildest fantasies. Could the dark clouds of the past years actually have a silver lining? The principal reassures me.

'Tanya, you have worked extremely hard and earned your place. I have no doubt that you will do well.'

My family and I had reached Tajikistan after a long and harrowing journey, exchanging the freezing cold of the Arctic north for the tropical heat of central Asia. To my dismay, by the time we arrived I had already missed the beginning of the school year, and anyway I was needed to help at home while Papa looked for work locally and further afield.

After several months, Papa had made enough money to engage a private tutor for me, a Jewish academic who had taught in a Polish university before the war. An elderly, balding man with thick glasses and a bushy mustache, he was a stern, but very interesting figure, and an excellent teacher. Throughout the summer months, I invested all my energies in study, spending several hours a day with 'the Professor', as I called him. His clear and concise presentation of the material prepared me well for the exams which I had to pass in order to be accepted into the final grade of senior school.

I struggled. The heat was oppressive and unrelenting, making concentration almost impossible. In the evenings, when there was some respite, I had to read by the dim light of a kerosene lamp since we had no electricity, and this quickly tired my eyes. The neighborhood in which we lived was bordered by fields and apple orchards, irrigated by water channels which flowed in close proximity to the houses. I would often take my books to a nearby grove, and study with my feet dangling in the cool water in an attempt to gain a little relief from the heat. The nights, too, were overwhelmingly hot. Sleeping indoors was impossible. Hauling my mattress up to the roof, I wrapped myself in netting for protection from the ever-hungry mosquitos and all manner of crawling insects, which emerged at night from their breeding ground in the irrigation channels. They buzzed annoyingly in my ears making sleep elusive, so that I was in a permanent a state of exhaustion. How could I possibly pass the exams?

With the Professor's encouragement and dedication I did pass, much to my surprise and delight, and I sailed through the final year of school with excellent grades, culminating in my meeting with the principal today.

Clutching the letter affirming my place at the university, I run home and burst into the house barely able to contain my excitement. And then I see that Papa's face wears an expression I have come to recognize only too well, whenever he is planning to uproot us. Before I have the chance to share my news, he declares, 'The war is over. It is time to go home.'

Chapter 2

Home - Nowy Sącz, Galicia, Poland, 1925-1939

My name is Tanya Anglische. I was born and raised in Nowy Sącz (pronounced Novi Sonts), where my parents set up home soon after they were married. The bustling city is the capital of the Krakow province, and one of the oldest towns in this part of Poland. Nestled between the Dunajec and Kamienica rivers, close to the border with Czechoslovakia, Nowy Sącz is located in a verdant valley surrounded by several mountain ranges, so in whichever direction you look, your eyes are greeted by picture postcard scenery.

Mama, Papa, I and my two younger brothers live in an apartment on the second floor of a two-story building, on a cobbled street a little way from the center of town. Most of the street's residents are gentiles, but our building's tenants are almost all Jewish. Nowy Sącz, or as it is known in Yiddish, Tsanz, boasts a long-standing Jewish presence beginning in the fifteenth century. The royal privilege of 1676 gave Jews the right to build their houses on the town's empty lots, and to engage in commerce and weaving. The seventeenth century Great Synagogue, situated in the old part of Tsanz, not far from the Town Hall, is renowned for its beautiful frescoes; and Tsanz is famous as the home of the revered eighteenth century Rabbi Chaim Halberstam, founder of the Tsanz Hassidic movement. By the time I was born, nearly one third of the town's residents were Jews, and a constant stream of countless more from throughout Europe making pilgrimages to the Rabbi's grave, injected a continental flavor into our provinciality.

Our landlord, Mr. Samuels, who lives on the ground floor with his family, is an impressive, portly gentleman, whose plump, generally smiling, face is framed by a dignified long beard flecked with grey. In addition to our building, he also owns an adjoining warehouse, where wood is stored, and a stable to house his two horses, cream-colored *Tancerz* and rust-brown *Shaynan*, that pull his delivery wagon. I love the clattering sound of the horses' heavy hooves and wagon's wheels, as they make their way along the cobbled street. Often, when I hear them approaching, I pilfer an apple or two from the pantry, and hurry down to spoil my adopted pets with a sweet treat.

The warehouse and stable provide perfect venues for playing hide-and-seek and other games with my friends, despite parental safety warnings, prohibitions and reprimands. We certainly try Mr. Samuels' patience, especially as we are always persuading his own children to join in with our antics, which wipes the smile off his face.

The front balcony of our apartment, decorated with an intricate wrought iron balustrade, overlooks the street, and commands a panoramic view towards the center of town, where Mama's parents live on the main thoroughfare, Jagiellonska Street. This busy street is lined with various businesses, including the main bank, a drogeria (pharmacy), and some fashionable stores. Among them stands my grandfather's delicatessen-cum-bakery and restaurant, which is considered to be the most highly-rated and elegant of Tsanz's kosher eateries.

I adore Grandfather, a tall, strong man, whose wide frame and muscular arms belie his gentle nature, warmth and generosity. He makes an impressive picture, standing in front of his store, greeting passers-by, who are lured inside by his persuasive patter and by the beckoning aroma of freshly baked goods. Whenever he sees me coming his way, he ushers me in and offers me warm, sweet *pierniczki*, savory *pierogi*, a soft drink, or something special from the restaurant's kitchen.

Grandfather is a charitable man, a man of *chesed*, good deeds. Behind his property live two destitute families, Faivish the cobbler and Anshel the carpenter, their wives, and a bevy of children. Every day, Grandfather makes sure they enjoy a hot meal by bringing them leftovers from the restaurant. He has also taken under his wing a feeble-minded man who has no family, remunerating him for simple tasks, such as deliveries and sweeping the street in front of the store's entrance.

Mama is one of nine children. Most of her close family lives here in Tsanz. Her siblings live in an apartment building not far from Grandfather's business, and many of my aunts and uncles help him in the store and in the restaurant. My grandparents live above their store. I'm ashamed to say that I'm not very fond of my grandmother, who always seems to be lying in bed or roaming the second floor apartment above the store in her housecoat. Mama has explained that she has a heart condition and requires rest. To me she just seems a fussy, spoilt and demanding woman. Whenever I visit she looks me up and down with a sour expression, and offers some criticism or other about my dress or my hair.

'Tanya, straighten your skirt. Pull down your sleeves. Your hair is untidy.' Everything has to be just so, and when I meet her I am required to kiss her hand and respectfully bob a small curtsey.

Papa's mother is a complete contrast to this stern woman, and I love her dearly. My paternal grandparents live in Tarnów, some sixty kilometers from Tsanz, so, regretfully, I don't get to see them very often. *'Little Bubbe'*, as I call her, is small in stature, with smiling grey-blue eyes and jet black hair, and she always wears a crisply starched white apron. She is warm and welcoming whenever I come to visit, and always has a small gift or other surprise for me.

The house in Tarnów is a veritable Aladdin's cave. In the salon, one glass case displays a treasure of coins; another is home to a collection of silver religious artifacts and other decorative objects. Papa's father, my *Zayde*, has a particular interest in timepieces, and owns some beautiful clocks, pocket and fob watches. Until recently, I was only allowed to look at them, but on my last visit Zayde let me handle some of them.

'Which one is your favorite, Tanya'leh?' he asked me.

'It's difficult to decide, Zayde,' I replied. 'There are so many lovely ones.'

I pointed to a pretty lady's fob watch, held by a blue enamel butterfly brooch. The back of the gold case was beautifully engraved with delicate flowers. The dial was white porcelain with black Roman numerals and blue hands. Another one which caught my eye was a silver fob watch, hanging from a filigree chain and enclosed in a case embossed with a cameo.

'Both excellent choices,' Zayde congratulated me. 'You have a good eye. They are both very special pieces.'

I basked in the warmth of his praise and affection.

Bubbe and Zayde's generous hospitality is well known. Every Sabbath they lay out a long table packed with free food and cakes for strangers from out of town, and for the local needy. Zayde owns a high-class patisserie, *Cukiernia Anglische*, offering mouth-watering eclairs, apple strudel, chocolate cakes and cheese cakes of every variety, cookies, and more. Customers come from all over to order specialty birthday and wedding cakes. Since Papa was expected to join the business, Zayde sent him to learn the trade from a well-known baker, a chocolatier and a confectioner. He travelled widely, gaining experience and ideas, but plans changed when he met Mama, and he did not settle in Tarnów, or take his place in Zayde's patisserie.

Papa's sister and two brothers also live in Tarnów, and they love to entertain me and take me on family outings in the area. The younger of the brothers, Hershel, has golden hands. Whenever he comes across discarded scraps of wood or metal, or broken items thrown away by their owners, he scoops them up and refashions them into something useful. When I was a small child he made me several wooden toys, which my brothers now play with. For my twelfth birthday, my *bat mitzvah*, he gave me a beautifully carved jewelry box. He has even built a gramophone and a radio. His sister, Miriam, is also good with her hands, and is employed as a senior seamstress in one of Tarnów's leading dressmaking establishments.

My best friend in Tsanz is Erna. She is as dark as a gypsy, with long, silky black hair down to her waist. She is beautiful and full of life. Her family of nine live in a neighboring apartment block, and she finds any excuse to get out and about, away from the cramped and noisy quarters. She happily helps me with the chores I have to undertake at the weekend, when our housekeeper has her days off. Her enthusiasm for this is boosted by the payment I give her in the form of candies and chocolate. These are a scarce commodity in her home, but plentiful in mine.

Perhaps this would be a good time to mention, in all modesty, that I am popular with both the Jewish and gentile children of the neighborhood. I would like to say that this is due to my outgoing, effervescent personality, but it would be unfair not to admit that it might have something to do with the fact that my father owns a candy factory. Children queue at *Anglishe Słodycze* for candies in the winter and ices in summer. Erna, being my special friend, is allowed to accompany me during vacation time to help out in the factory. Our favorite station is at the popsicle assembly line, where Papa entrusts us with the task of blowing open the colorful paper wrappers with a short, sharp puff, and quickly inserting the ices before they have a chance to melt. Our favorites are the ones coated in a layer of chocolate before wrapping. On a break, we each take one and dip it over and over again into the hot dark liquid, until the layer of chocolate is almost as thick as the ice cream underneath it. In winter, however, we are unemployed.

Papa does not let us help in the candy-making process, because he worries that the boiling sugar is too much of a hazard. I don't put up an argument, because I have been witness to numerous occasions when he has come home bandaged after a mishap in the factory.

The balcony at the rear of our apartment overlooks 'Venice', an enormous park so nicknamed because it is scattered with a myriad of lakes and rivulets. In summer, these are swollen by snow melt, and the water beckons invitingly, becoming a bathing paradise and magnet for picnickers. In winter, *Venice*'s largest lake, which freezes over, serves as an ice-rink, a sparkling mirror alive with the swirling hues of colorful coats and scarves, and shards of sunlight reflected brightly off skates, as people of all ages dance and twirl in delight. Erna and I spend hours on the ice, perfecting our skills. When we get tired or bored, we run home for a cup of hot chocolate and a slice of whichever cake Mama has brought home from Grandfather's store.

In spring, when the trees and flowers began to return to life, townsfolk stroll leisurely through the park, savoring the seasonal rejuvenation and fresh air perfumed by fragrant apple and yellow linden blossom. On Saturdays, the Jewish Sabbath, when activity in the park is particularly lively, Erna and I like to sit on my balcony and watch the passers-by, inventing fictitious biographies for them. For example, pointing towards a clump of trees, I might tell Erna, 'You see that mountain of a man with wild hair and an unkempt beard? He is a hunter who keeps fierce animals on his balcony. He has a wolf and a bear and he is roaming the park looking for squirrels and other sweetmeats for their dinner.'

Not to be outdone, Erna might counter with, 'That colorful fellow with the feathered hat and slender hands is an artist, who has been commissioned to paint a portrait of the Mayor's mistress.'

Our fabrications keep us endlessly amused.

Young couples, holding hands and smiling lovingly at each other, particularly catch our attention. One particular Saturday afternoon is etched in my memory. Scanning the park, I singled out a pretty blond girl and her beau, hands clasped and looking longingly at each other with doe eyes.

Erna turned to me and said, 'You realize that they do much more than just holding hands, don't you?'

Naively intrigued I asked, 'You mean kissing?'

My parents are not demonstrative, but, of course, I have witnessed the odd peck on the cheek, a warm embrace or intimate smile. Erna, however, appeared to be very knowledgeable about such things. She began to enlighten me.

'Have you never seen a penis?' she asked incredulously.

'I have two baby brothers, of course I have seen it,' I replied indignantly, but my eyes grew wider as she began to elaborate on alternative functions of this seemingly harmless little organ, and on the intricacies of sexual relationships. Engrossed in these new discoveries, we did not notice Mama step out onto the balcony.

'I thought you girls might like some refreshments,' she said, laying out sour milk and black bread slathered with fresh butter.

Looking at my blushing cheeks inquisitively, she asked, 'What is all this giggling and whispering about?'

Mama, who already disapproved of my friendship with Erna, would have banned her from the house indefinitely had she overhead our conversation, or discovered our reading habits. Erna's oldest sister is an avid reader of romance fiction, and from time to time Erna manages to 'borrow' one her novels for us to read in secret. My friend is certainly giving me an education I would not have received from anyone else at my age.

My more conventional education is conducted in the town's

Hebrew elementary school. Poland has had a checkered history of antisemitism, alternating between religious persecution, on the one hand, and the recognition of the rich commercial and cultural contribution the Jews could make to Polish society on the other. Under the Russian and Austro-Hungarian Empires, Polish Jews were heavily persecuted and pogroms were condoned. In the aftermath of World War I, however, the Constitution of Independent Poland gave the Jews the same legal rights as other citizens and guaranteed them religious tolerance. In Tsanz, two Jewish schools and a yeshiva were established, and today Jewish youth and religious groups, diverse political parties and Zionist organizations, newspapers and theater all flourish.

The school I attend is a private establishment set up by the local Zionist organization, *Tarbut*. All the studies are taught in Hebrew, except for Polish language and history. The school, officially recognized by the Polish authorities, has an enrollment of one hundred students. Overt antisemitism is not palpable on the streets of Tsanz, although in recent years there have been several incidents of assaults on Jewish stores. Jews are not ghettoized, and, although we choose to live in close proximity to each other, we mix freely with our gentile neighbors. Recently, however, I have overheard my parents and their friends discussing how the times are changing, and that antisemitism is on the rise. This is also reflected in the mantra of my school: '*Next year in Jerusalem.*' Our sights are set on the Holy Land, *Eretz Israel*. Since the Balfour Declaration in 1917, the Zionist dream of the creation of the State of Israel has been seen as the future reality.

It's late spring 1939, towards the end of the school year, and I have to sit exams for entry into secondary school, the *gimnazjium*. I want to continue to a Hebrew school, but the nearest good one is in Krakow, over one hundred kilometers away, and my parents will not hear of it. Our town has recently witnessed an influx of German refugees, and unsettling rumors are rife that Jews are being rounded up and sent to German labor camps.

'In times such as these,' insists Papa, 'families stay together.'

Most of my friends have tried out for the local school, but my mother, in a fit of snobbism, decided to register me for a select private school in town where, in addition to matriculation studies, students are offered art, fashion design, and other subjects. The day of the examination arrives, and I approach the school in nervous trepidation. It is housed in a former palace, an enormous structure in the baroque style. At the entrance, I'm told to remove my shoes, replacing them with special slippers which, it is explained, won't mark the huge, once luxuriant but now faded, carpets which cover the parquet floor. Directly ahead a sweeping staircase ascends to an upper gallery, adorned by what was once an ornately carved balustrade, but which is now chipped, peeling and lusterless. The whole building smells of neglect and disrepair, and it would take every ounce of my imagination to conjure up a picture of its former splendor.

I'm led along a corridor and ushered into a large room on the ground floor, where I am directed to a lone chair facing a panel of examiners.

'State your name,' demands a formidable, white-haired gentleman seated directly opposite me.

'Tanya Anglische, Sir,' I reply, trying to disguise the tremble in my voice.

'I see you have achieved excellent grades and your teachers give a positive account of your character and behavior. Please tell us why you wish to attend this school'

I can't tell them that actually I would prefer to be going elsewhere, or that my mother has high aspirations for me, so I fumble for a reply which I hope will satisfy. Mama's words ring in my ears as I remember how she argued to convince my father that this was the right decision.

'I would appreciate having the opportunity to broaden my

horizons in the direction of the arts, and to study with pupils and teachers I have not been acquainted with since kindergarten.'

Several of the other members of the panel ask me some simple questions, and then the ordeal is over. The panel members confer amongst themselves, discussing me as if I'm not in the room. I must have lied convincingly enough because the white-haired gentleman finally announces that they are pleased to offer me a place.

When I meet with my classmates the following day I find out that they have been less fortunate. Not one of them has passed the exams for the local *gimnazjium*. When I ask what happened, one friend tells me, 'Most of the questions were simple and straightforward, but then, we were asked to recite the last lines of the Polish national anthem.'

The anthem is extremely long, and usually no one sings the last verse, certainly not in our Hebrew school. This task was deliberately designed to trip them up and exclude them from entry. It is a clear warning of an alarming shift in the status quo.

Chapter 3

Summer, 1939

As summer of 1939 arrives, my classmates and I finish elementary school. A party is organized to celebrate this milestone, but the atmosphere is heavy, not only because many of us are going separate ways, but also because there is a feeling of impending uncertainty. There is something unpleasant in the air. War is in the air. Jew hatred is in the air. The Germans have already taken Silesia and are advancing on Sudetenland. That puts them firmly on our doorstep.

At the party, our favorite teacher, Mr. Koplinsky, addresses us solemnly.

'This may be our last meeting. Perhaps we will be scattered around the world like leaves in the wind, and never see each other again. Let us remember our roots and from whence we came. Do not forget our traditions, and our yearning to be in the Land of Israel. If we ever meet again, let it be there.'

Despite the growing anxiety, my family takes the train up into the mountains to Szczwanica, as we do every year for our summer vacation. I am the oldest of three siblings. My brother Jozef is eight, five years my junior, and the baby, Dovid, is four years younger still. The two boys have looked forward to this journey with palpable anticipation. On days when they test her patience, Mama often sits them by our apartment window, which looks out in the direction of the railway tracks, so that they can be distracted and entertained by watching the fast trains whizz by on their way to cities near and far, or up to the ski villages and spas in the mountains. They compete to see who gets the first glimpse of the tell-tale billowing white smoke, which heralds the imminent approach of a train. Four tracks pass through the station, so they never have to wait very long. They are so excited now that it's their turn to board our vacation train. How could any of us know that soon our train journeys would be the stuff of nightmares and not of dreams?

As the train clambers and lurches its way up towards the peaceful beauty of the mountains, a holiday atmosphere pervades the carriage. But, unlike my brothers, I can sense an undercurrent of tension, and see the barely disguised looks of anxiety that pass between my parents. The uphill journey lasts barely an hour. Our destination is nestled in a picturesque mountain setting, surrounded by lush vegetation and the rushing waters of the Grajcarek River. From a distance, the mountains appear to be covered by one uniform green forest, but as we draw nearer I can make out nuances of shape and hue, distinguishing the majestic, pyramid-shaped spruce, which seems to touch the sky, from its neighboring shorter fir, whose delicate needles hang down like lacy curtains. The higher peaks are rugged and bare, having been covered in snow throughout the winter. Dotted here and there, large patches of grassy meadow host a solitary farmhouse, or a lonely church, whose steeple peeks out among the trees. The crisp air is laced with the heady scent of pine, and the rural silence is punctuated by the distant chiming of cow bells.

Szczawnica is the most famous spa center in Poland, named for the acidic waters – *szczawy* – whose medicinal properties have been recognized for hundreds of years. Its thermal baths, and unique *Inhalatorium*, specializing in the treatment of lung diseases, attract tourists from all over Europe. The town boasts several hotels and guesthouses. The central square, which is actually more of a circle, is graced by a pretty fountain, overlooked by a statue of a woman with small children, and surrounded by neatly cultivated beds of brightly colored flowers.

Every summer, Papa rents the same cottage in a remote spot, well away from the hustle and bustle of the town's busy center, much to our childish delight but to the chagrin of Mama. She would relish the opportunity to rub shoulders with some of the fashionable tourists, and eye their outfits, as they take refreshments in the outdoor coffee houses, or stroll leisurely along the paved promenade in the fresh mountain air.

Once we are settled in our small, but clean and functional cottage, Papa takes the train back to Nowy Sącz. He will return to join us at the weekends, bringing food supplies and other necessities, and treats of sweets and chocolates. To Mama he also brings news from town, but this is kept for hushed whispers after we children are tucked up in bed.

In the mornings, we are roused by the high-pitched voice of the neighboring farmer's wife, Helenka. Mama hands me three large mugs and sends me outside with Jozef and Dovid. Helenka is waiting on the doorstep with her goat, Wanda, named for one of the town's mineral water sources. Working Wanda's udders fiercely, Helenka milks her directly into our mugs. We are made to drink the warm, rather smelly milk immediately, since Mama says it's a cure for all manner of ills. Every year, the first few mugsful make me *feel* ill, but as the days go by I become accustomed to the taste and smell. This summer I have decided that I will ask Helenka to teach me how to do the milking myself.

It's my job to keep Jozef and Dovid entertained and out of mischief. Days pass in a leisurely fashion, with walks along the many wooded paths, and swimming in the calmer, shallower waters of the creeks and streams, which trickle into the more violent torrents of the river below. I take my brothers on foraging expeditions to find wild strawberries and ripening cranberries. We gather fragrant posies of yarrow and cornflowers for Mama, and collect pine cones of different shapes and sizes. The boys, being boys, also hunt for caterpillars, ladybugs, and whatever other insects they can find.

Some days we wander a little further. and sit quietly by the river watching anglers fishing in the clear waters. Occasionally, one of them lets me or Jozef hold the fishing rod, and gives us a lesson in how to cast the line out into the water. Mama is delighted if we are given a fish or two to take home for dinner. And in the evening, I tell the boys the folk tale of *The Fisherman and the Magic Fish*.

The boys love to hear stories from Polish and Yiddish folklore. Both cultures are rich in tales of magic and mystery, wizards and wonder-working rabbis, damsels in distress and *dybbuks*. Most of these are spine-chillingly frightening for small boys; the Wawel fire-eating dragon and the Golem of Prague make them shudder. At bedtime I have to make up my own gentler stories to lull them into sleep. I admit that I carry out my babysitting mission reluctantly, missing Erna, and wishing she was here so that we could spend our time more adventurously. As soon as the boys are quiet, I sit outside on the porch and write letters to her, for Papa to deliver when he returns to town after the weekend. All week I wait in anticipation for her reply.

One day in the middle of the vacation, Mama takes us into town to see the locals' special folklore festival. They are mostly shepherds and highlanders, and in honor of the festivities they dress in traditional costume. Both the men and women wear crisp, snow-white, puffed-sleeved shirts, but the men's are teamed with richly embroidered waistcoats in blue or green, while the women's outfits are red pinafore dresses with white lace aprons. There is a dance troupe accompanied by a small band, playing traditional folk tunes, and the spectators clap along enthusiastically. Mama lets us wander from stall to stall to admire the displays of handicrafts, and, as a special treat, we climb aboard a Dorożką (horse drawn carriage) which takes us on a circuit around town. It's a perfect day, worlds apart from the stressful situation we left back in Tsanz.

Just before the beginning of the school year, Papa comes to take us home as usual. On the way down the mountain I read Erna's final letter. She writes, 'Something's going to happen. An entire military battalion has been brought to town. The barracks are packed with soldiers. The school is also full of them. It looks like the opening of the school year is definitely in doubt.'

Erna is right. The day I'm supposed to start my new fancy school comes and goes, and I'm at home, looking after my brothers. Suddenly, I hear an unfamiliar caterwauling sound outside. I venture out on to the balcony and peer across towards the railway tracks, where I see a man waving his arms frantically. I can make out a plane flying overhead. I hear some shots and in an instant the man crumples to the ground. I gasp as realization hits me; the ghastly rise-and-fall wail must be an air-raid siren. I run back inside, grab Jozef and Dovid by the hand, and drag them down the stairs to the basement. Huddled together and shaking with fear, I silently pray for Mama who has gone to the market, and for Papa who is at the factory. One word spins around and around in my head – *War*.

When all seems quiet, we creep cautiously back upstairs, and collide with Mama as she bursts in looking disheveled and breathing heavily.

'There is such pandemonium and panic at the market,' she tells us in a shaking voice, with tears streaming down her face.

'Planes flew low and strafed the stalls, sending produce flying every which way. People scattered in every direction, and some were hit. I didn't look back; I just ran for my life. I barely made it home.'

Almost immediately, Papa arrives to check that we are all safe.

'I am going to Grandfather's to try to get a news update on his radio.'

He opens the door to leave, only to find Grandfather standing there, with a grave expression on his face.

'The news is bad,' he tells us. 'The Germans have invaded Poland. The situation is deteriorating rapidly. Rumors abound of bombings, and that the Germans are advancing on our town.'

Mama tries to calm the boys, while Grandfather and Papa stand to one side, discussing what's to be done. They collect up all of our valuables, and lock them away in the basement. Suddenly, there is a soft knock at the door. It's Papa's good friend, Karol, a gentile who owns a nearby bakery.

'My friend,' I overhear him whisper to Papa, 'The Germans are murdering every Jew in their path. It's not safe for you here. You must flee the town, and speed is of the essence. The garrisoned Polish soldiers are planning to blow up all the bridges over the Dunajec River in order to stop the Germans reaching the city. But this will also prevent citizens from leaving.'

The next day Grandfather helps my Grandmother and two of my aunts onto the train to Tarnów. Tarnów is further from the border and from the German army, and he reasons that they will be safer there with Papa's family. This mission accomplished, he tells us that he is going to look for some means of transportation to take us away. After some time he returns. It's obvious from the look on his face that he has not been successful.

'This is a hopeless exercise. There's not even a horse and cart to be had in all of Tsanz.'

Four days after the German invasion of Poland, under cover of darkness, and with no other choice, we leave home on foot. Papa explains that our escape necessitates traveling light, without the luxury of luggage. It's already impossible to withdraw cash from the bank, so he has taken whatever money was in the factory's safe, and Mama's housekeeping money, her jewelry and a few other small valuables.

'Tanya,' Mama instructs me, 'wear three dresses and a sweater under your coat. This way you will have a change of clothing and something warm to wear once the weather becomes colder.'

Surely we will be back home long before winter, I tell myself. But I do what I'm told.

Just before dawn, our family leaves Tsanz, the only home I've ever known. Mama and Papa, Grandfather, me, eight-year old Jozef and four year old Dovid, make our way across one of the last remaining bridges over the Dunajec River. When we reach the other side, we stop and turn around to breathe in a last glimpse of the town, as dawn begins to cast a dim light on the church steeples and the ancient castle. Solemnly, we turn away to begin our journey. We have progressed only a short distance when we hear a massive explosion, and the ground shakes as the bridge behind us disintegrates and sinks slowly into the river.

Chapter 4

On the Road

We have walked a few kilometers when a wagon passes by. The driver takes pity on Grandfather and offers him a ride. Hoisting little Dovid up to the wagon, Grandfather climbs up beside him, pulls him on to his lap, and the old man and young child jog along harmoniously for a little way. Dovid is delighted with this new experience, calling 'giddy-up' to the horses and mimicking the sound of their hooves on the road. Mama is relieved to have some peace.

We are not alone on the road. In front of us and behind courses a stream of people, young, middle-aged, and elderly adults, children, babies, and even pets. From afar they look to all intents and purposes as if they are out for pleasant stroll in the countryside. But, on closer inspection, the terror and uncertainty emanating from their manner is almost palpable, and the fear in their eyes reflects my own.

Suddenly, the air begins to vibrate with the noise of approaching airplanes. Papa shouts at us to run to the ditch at the side of the road and take cover. Within seconds the planes are swooping down and firing randomly at the people on the road. Can they not see that these are just ordinary families, women and children? There are no soldiers, no uniforms, no orderly marching or army vehicles. Horrified, I realize that this is just target practice.

When the attack ceases, and the noise of the planes has dissipated into the distance, we tentatively make our way back up onto the road. The scene before me is surreal. The road, which, until a few moments ago, heaved with fleeing families, is now littered with dead and wounded. An overturned cart has spewed its contents in every direction. One wheel spins aimlessly, while the other pins down a wounded horse, whose eyes wide with fear stare glassily at nothing. Acrid smoke billows skywards, and the settling dust mingles with rivulets of blood. Turning aside, Mama covers the boys' eyes shielding them from the gruesome tableau, but the wailing and screaming can't be blotted out.

I stand riveted to the spot in stunned silence. This is not my first encounter with death, and the scene sparks an unhappy memory. Every summer, the winter ice rink in our *Venice* park serves as a boating lake. A couple of years ago, a group of us were sailing on the lake when one of my neighbors, Tomasz, who liked to show off, claimed that he could swim from one side of the lake to the other. With much pomp and ceremony, he dived off the boat into the lake, but he didn't resurface. Did he intend to swim the whole way underwater? We all scanned the lake but there was no sign of him. We called for help, but it was already too late. Tomasz's head had been sucked into the rich sludge on the lake's bottom. When they pulled him out, he was already dead. He was an only child and it was a terrible tragedy. I had nightmares for weeks, reliving the image of his pale, lifeless body and the heartrending cries of his bereft parents.

I was snapped out of my reverie by Papa.

'Come, Tanya'leh. We must keep moving. It's too dangerous to stay in one spot.'

We continue walking through the afternoon and into the night. Although we are all desperate to stop and rest, Papa insists we keep going until late into the morning on the following day. About twenty kilometers from Tsanz we come to the small town of Bobowa. Papa makes inquiries, and learns that at the local station we will be able to catch a train to Tarnów, to be reunited with Grandmother and the rest of the family.

Mama finds a small store where she buys some refreshments, and we sit down in the station to wait for the train. Suddenly, Grandfather stands up.

'I must go and pay respects to the revered Bobowa Rabbi, and receive his blessing for the family. I will not be gone long.'

And despite our pleas to the contrary, he walks away, charging me to look after his coat and prayer shawl until his return.

Hours pass but there is no sign of a train or of Grandfather. Then, towards evening, a freight train pulls slowly into the station. It's brimming with fleeing Jews who urge us to get aboard.

'This is the last train,' they insist. 'If you miss this one you will be stranded here.'

Papa paces to and fro, weighed down by the dilemma of what to do. Should we wait for Grandfather who has not yet returned, or should we take the train? Finally, he makes his decision.

'It is my responsibility to save my family. We must get on the train.'

'Papa, no,' I beg him. 'Grandfather is also family. I won't leave without him.'

But Papa is steadfast in his resolve.

'Grandfather wouldn't wish us to miss this opportunity because of him. He is a resourceful man and he will find a way to reach Grandmother in Tarnów.'

Drawing me close so that he can whisper in my ear, he tells me, 'From now on, Tanya'leh, we must live by the three esses rule.'

In answer to my puzzled expression he explains, 'Three esses: *Shelter, Sustenance, Survival.*'

So, clutching Grandfather's coat and prayer shawl close to my heavy heart, I follow the others and reluctantly board the already crowded train.

As it transpires, the train is not even traveling in the direction of Tarnów, but is heading east. The trucks are laden with coal, and the moment we embark we are covered in fine black soot, which infiltrates every nook and cranny. The passengers are refugees, and I now realize that this is to be my new status too, until we settle in a new home or return to Tsanz. Perhaps I'm naïve and optimistic, but I'm certain that this will only be a short-lived hiatus in my normal life.

The train rattles along the tracks, the *clickety-clack* of its wheels soothing my little brothers, and lulling them into peaceful sleep. Whenever the train slows as it passes through a small hamlet or next to a farm, some of the locals take pity on us, and proffer food and water. This fills the emptiness in my stomach, but it can't fill the void in my spirit created by Grandfather's absence. The first night I cry myself to sleep, hugging his abandoned possessions, and dream I can hear his voice, smell his special smell. I'm miserable and terrified of what might befall him.

We eventually draw into the city of Lwow, on the Ukranian border, where Papa discovers the journey is terminating. The very moment we disembark, the now familiar sound of an air raid siren gives us a deafening welcome and sends chills up my spine. The Luftwaffe seems to be stalking us, predicting our every move. Most of our fellow passengers are making a run towards a splendid-looking hotel standing opposite the station, in order to take cover. Papa says he has no strength or desire to run with the herd.

'The train tracks are likely to be the planes' primary target,' he says. 'We will take shelter in the station house.'

Pulling us next to a wall in a corner of the building, he tells us to huddle down. We have barely taken up our position when the bombing begins. What a fearsome noise! Somehow, being inside makes the explosions sound even louder than the previous attack, when we were out in the open. Bombs whistle down, pounding their targets with jarring blasts, followed by the thunder of collapsing brickwork. The station shakes as if an earthquake has hit it. My entire body trembles. Amazingly, I'm not so scared for myself, but rather for my family. I can't stomach the thought of losing my parents or brothers. It's enough that I have already lost Grandfather.

The sound of the bombing stops as quickly as it began, and is replaced by an eerie stillness. We get to our feet and brush ourselves off, dusty, but thankfully unscathed. But the sight that meets our eyes is devastating. The hotel which minutes ago had stood so majestically in front of the station has been completely razed to the ground, and all those who took shelter within are buried alive. Suddenly, the silence is pierced by the cries of the injured and the wailing of those whose loved ones are dead in the street or missing in the rubble.

In a matter of seconds, the mournful cries are joined by the wailing of a fire engine's siren. The air is thick with smoke and dust, and Papa tells us to cover our noses and mouths. Debris is lying all around; broken glass glints in the sun, and scorched towels are flying like kites around the ruins. My gaze fixes on the sorry sight of an orphaned doll and a headless teddy bear lying next to a single shoe. The hotel signage, which has somehow survived the blast, has come to rest at an angle on the pavement, and its neon lights are flashing erratically, sending sparks in every direction. A double bed is standing bizarrely in the middle of the road, and a miraculously unscathed chandelier is hanging proudly from the telephone cable overhead. My attention is caught by a shower of feathers wafting in the wind.

'Oh no, Papa,' I cry. 'The explosion must have hit a flock of birds.'

Papa follows my gaze.

'No, Tanya'leh. Those are feathers from the hotel's pillows and eiderdowns.'

Mama is staring in shock at the appalling scene, and the boys are crying pitifully. Shaking with fear and grief, I hug myself closely into Papa's side for comfort and protection.

Looking heavenwards he says, 'Once again we have been spared.'

I inwardly pray that it's not Grandfather who is watching over us from above and keeping us safe.

'It's clear that it is not safe to remain in Lwow.' Papa announces. 'My instinct tells me that rather than trying to reach Tarnów, we should keep going eastwards away from the advancing Germans.'

However, it's not clear when, or if, an eastbound train would arrive. So, having no choice, several hours later Papa herds us on to the first train that arrives at the station. Unfortunately, it's heading back in the direction of Poland from where we have come. After about an hour, we suddenly pull to a standstill as we approach the station at Sudova Vyshnya. On the parallel track stands a train packed with soldiers and munitions.

'Get off the train immediately,' one of them shouts, waving his arms. 'German planes are coming. Run as fast as you can!'

I can't believe this is happening again. Are the German pilots deliberately following us from place to place, tormenting us with a game of cat and mouse? Is my particular family locked in their crosshairs, and they won't be satisfied until the target is obliterated?

Papa grabs our small bag and a few of our other bits and pieces, and pushes us from the train. As Mama jumps down one of her high heels breaks off. Half running, half limping, she presents a comic picture, and despite the circumstances the boys and I giggle at the ridiculous spectacle. A small copse borders one side of the tracks, and we make our way there. Papa spreads us out, each under the shelter of a separate tree, explaining that he doesn't want to risk us being one single target. I cringe as the meaning of his strategy registers. If only one or two of us are hit, at least some of the family will be left alive.

The tree trunks aren't particularly thick or sturdy, and I can't believe that they will provide sufficient protection. I look to the side and realize that I am not alone under my tree. On the other side of it crouches a young soldier, and I'm aghast to see tears spilling from his eyes bright with fear, and rolling slowly down his cheeks. He looks as if he is only a couple of years older than me, a boy in an ill-fitting uniform, thrust unwillingly into the horrors of war.

And it begins. Black swastikas glint with bravado in the sunlight as the planes swoop down from the sky, flying low and strafing everything in their path. The noise of exploding bombs and the rat-ta-tat of the machine guns is deafening. Bullets whoosh past me, and I can see little potholes in the ground where they have landed only a stone's throw from where I am sheltering. My soldier and I huddle down even further, and cover our ears to blot out the sound. The planes come around for a second attack, just to be sure, and then hurtle off to their next mission.

Once again, all is quiet. I have become almost as scared of this after-silence as I am of the attacks themselves. I look towards the tracks. The train is on fire, and passengers who didn't manage to disembark before the raid are dead or dying. Others who didn't reach cover in time have been cut down as they ran. The screams are deafening, and to my horror, I realize that the loudest are mine. Panicking, I search around for Papa and Mama and the boys. My prayers are answered; we are all in one piece. And then, I turn to my soldier. His head droops to one side and blood pours from his ears. Uncontrollable sobs rack my body and I can barely stop myself from retching. How can it be that the minute distance separating us has saved my life but taken his? He is so young, has not even seen battle, and yet is already a casualty of war.

Apart from the few things that Papa snatched from the train, all our possessions have gone up in smoke. The journey from Lwow had been stiflingly hot, and I had removed two of my dresses. They are now ashes, as are Grandfather's coat and prayer shawl. Mama is examining the damage to her shoe, when Papa, in a fit of anger which I have never before witnessed in this placid man, grabs them, breaks the heel off the undamaged one, and throws them back at her.

'Who in their right mind tries to flee the Nazis wearing high-heeled shoes?' he barks derisively.

It is a measure of the fear he is trying to hide.

We are all traumatized, exhausted, hungry and thirsty, and desperate for a wash after two days on the road. A sorry band of homeless refugees, we walk on, and after a short distance we arrive at a small village, where Papa hopes we will find food and a place to rest.

The local Jews of the village are welcoming, and a family generously gives us a room with a huge bed. After food and a wash, we all clamber in together, and snuggle under the huge eiderdown quilt. But it reminds me of the floating feathers in Lwow. Despite the comfort and exhaustion, my fears make sleep elusive. I listen to the boys' soft breathing and my parents' gentle snoring. Eventually, I doze, but nightmarish images from the past few days haunt me, and my sleep is restless.

Chapter 5

Wandering Jews

The following morning our host takes Papa aside.

'It's not safe for you or for any of us to stay here. The Germans are constantly bombing. We are leaving for the next village where we know a Jewish farmer who will give us shelter. You should come with us.'

So we set off again, and walk the few kilometers to the next village.

The farmer greets us warmly but apologizes to Papa, 'I'm afraid that there's no space in the farmhouse for two additional families, but you are welcome to stay in our barn.'

He gives us some blankets and helps Papa organize makeshift beds of hay. The boys and I jump around on them as if on a trampoline. The hay gets stuck in our hair and on our clothes and soon we look like scarecrows. The hay tickles our noses and little Dovid has a sneezing fit, which makes us all laugh, lightening the tense atmosphere.

The farmer's wife, Gittel, invites us in for a warm meal, and the boys play happily with Ezra, a friendly sheepdog, that basks contentedly in the unexpected attention of these newfound visitors. At sundown we say goodnight and return to the barn. The boys are overexcited about this novel camping adventure and are difficult to settle. Eventually, tiredness overcomes their excitement, and we can all finally snuggle down for the night.

We are rudely awakened early the next morning by the sound of approaching aircraft. There is no siren here to warn of an imminent air raid, but the farmer's flock of geese raises an ear-deafening commotion, honking in unison as they sense the danger. The farmer runs into the barn.

'The geese are alerting us to take cover. There's no air raid shelter here. The best you can do is to bury yourselves in the piles of hay.'

The boys cling to me and Mama in fear. Having already experienced the recent bombings, they know what to expect. As we take cover, I pray that the Germans have more important targets than an isolated farm. The planes pass over us, no doubt saving their ammunition for attacks on the surrounding towns and villages, where, according to the farmer, harsh battles are already being fought between German and Polish forces. This time my prayers are answered.

Once the danger has passed, Papa gathers us together.

'I think we'll be safer if we put more distance between us and the Germans. We'll stay here for another day or two and then move on.'

We pack up our few belongings, and Gittel gives us some food for the way. Retracing our steps, we make our way back to Sudova Vyshnya, where we had last disembarked from the train. Mama and Papa knock on a few doors, hoping a kind family will take us in. They have no luck for quite some time, but then a gracious widow, Hannah, welcomes us into the home she shares with her two sons. I sigh with relief when I see that in this building there is an air raid shelter to protect us.

For several days all remains quiet, and then one night, the sounds of battle, the pounding of cannons, and the rat-ta-tat of machine guns, seem to be close by. The following morning our worst fears are realized. German voices in the street are shouting '*Raus Juden.* Out Jews.'

Petrified, we emerge with the other few families who have taken shelter in our building, to face the enemy. To our amazement they don't intend to harm us, but merely demand that we hand over all the food in our possession. It seems they are starving, and are willing to spare us for a loaf of bread and other supplies.

The noise of battle continues night after night. Sometimes the Polish soldiers advance on the town, and the next day they are forced to retreat. After several more days, the Polish army is finally trounced.

'This will be bad for us,' says Papa, not even attempting to hide his anxiety.

'It means that the Germans are here to stay, and this time I don't believe they will be lenient with us.'

Sure enough, the following day an announcement by a Nazi officer is made in the marketplace.

'You have been defeated. We are now in charge. All Jewish men will report here for work tomorrow morning.'

Papa says that there is no point in hiding.

'It will be worse for us if we are caught.' So the next day he leaves the apartment together with Hannah's two sons.

I stay with Mama and the boys, but after a while the uncertainty of what has happened to Papa overwhelms me.

'I can't just sit here,' I tell Mama. 'I'm going to find him.'

And before she can stop me, I dash out and go in search of him. In the distance I can hear a commotion coming from the direction of the town center, so I make my way there. The sight that meets my eyes is a distressing one. The center of town is marked by a large cobbled square, bordered by the municipal building and a church. In one corner of the square I can see a German officer standing on a podium, barking orders and insults at a group of men, including my father. The middle of the square is occupied by a tank. Papa and the others have been ordered to clean it. Each man is holding a metal helmet to which a rope is attached, and they are using these to draw water from a nearby well. Having no other equipment, they are forced to scrub the filth off the tank with their bare hands and fingernails. Many have already drawn blood, which mingles with the dirt and stains their faces as they wipe sweat off their brows and out of their eyes.

Tears fill my eyes as I watch Papa's humiliation, but this is not the only thing that appalls me. For the first time in my life I am witness to the true colors of the local Poles. They stand pointing at the men, clapping and jeering, shouting venomous insults, goading them to work harder and faster. Not only does no one lift a finger to protest or help them, they are actually entertained by the grotesque travesty. I turn and run back to Mama and the boys before Papa notices me.

'Well?' asks Mama as I come through the door. 'Did you find Papa?'

Wanting to spare her unnecessary anguish, I put on a brave face and answer, 'Yes, Mama. He is fine. He is just doing some cleaning work with the other men.'

In the evening, Papa comes home exhausted and broken. He does not even attempt to spare our feelings.

'They want to kill us,' he says, wearily. 'At this rate it won't take them long.'

For the next few days he leaves early in the morning and returns home in the evening barely able to stand. Then, one morning he announces, 'Grandfather came to me in a dream. He urged me to run away before it's too late. He said we would all die here, and that we must leave this place.'

He tells us that he has become friendly with another member of the work gang, a Mr. Frenkel, who comes from Przemyśl (*pronounced Pshemisshel*), a large town about twenty-five kilometers away.

'Apparently, he had the misfortune to be trapped in Sudova Vyshnya on his way home from a business trip, and he is desperate to get back to his family,' Papa tells us.

'Mr. Frenkel and I have hatched a plan to bribe a local farmer who will smuggle us out of town.'

When the arrangements are in place, Papa tries to persuade our landlady Hannah to leave with us, but to no avail.

'My sons are young and strong, and can survive the hard work. I am sure the Germans will get bored soon enough and leave us alone. What would they want with an old woman, anyway?' she argues.

Our escape necessitates breaking the curfew imposed by the Germans from dusk to dawn. Anyone caught out in the street after dark faces severe consequences, and this makes the first part of our escape particularly hazardous. Luckily, Hannah's apartment is quite near to the outskirts of town, and moving fast and low, we leave the town behind us quite quickly, and reach the pre-arranged rendezvous where our farmer-cum-smuggler awaits us. While he buries Papa and Mr. Frenkel under piles of hay on the back of his wagon, Mama and I disguise ourselves and the boys, by dressing up in some peasants' clothes that he has brought for us. Wearing a colorful babushka kerchief on her head, Mama sits next to the farmer on the driver's seat. We children are told to lie down on top of the hay and pretend to be asleep. The laden cart begins to move as two heavy horses pull slowly away.

The road is empty and the silence is only broken by the clip-clop of the horses' hooves. The farmer begins to whistle a happy tune, as if we are simply on a family outing in the countryside. All seems to be going to plan, and then, after a little while, a barely audible noise pierces the early morning stillness.

'Mama,' I whisper. 'Do you hear the distant rumbling of an engine coming from the direction in which we are heading?'

The noise grows louder and louder as it approaches us, until I can make out a convoy of three army jeeps carrying soldiers. As they near the cart, the jeeps slow down, and I find myself face to face with German soldiers, the collars of their distinctive grey uniforms brandishing the SS rune, which looks to me like double bolts of lightning. I am holding my breath in fear but manage a sweet, innocent smile. Haughtily, they give us no more than a cursory look up and down. It seems an old farmer with a woman and children are not worthy of their time or interest, and they speed off to carry out their business in Sudova Vyshnya.

It's afternoon by the time we reach the outskirts of Przemyśl. Stopping beside the cart, a gentile, who apparently has greater expertise than the SS in recognizing Jews when he sees them, asks derisively, 'Where are you headed, Jews? To Przemyśl? Yesterday they rounded up and killed hundreds of Jews, men, women and children.' With a hint of satisfaction in his voice he adds, 'It's not safe for you there. Be on your way.'

Mr. Frenkel is alarmed, and desperate to find his wife and daughter alive and well.

Since going back to Sudova Vyshnya is not an option, we have little choice but to continue on with Mr. Frenkel. We get down from the cart, helping the men brush off the hay which has stuck to their clothing. Mr. Frenkel pays the farmer and bids him goodbye, and then suggests, 'Let's look for a secluded place to have a picnic. We are hungry and thirsty and we don't dare try to get into Przemyśl until nightfall, even though it means breaking curfew once again.'

Registering Mama's fearful expression, he assures her, 'I was born and raised in the town. I know all the back alleys by which we will circumvent the center, where the Germans are most likely stationed.'

We stay hidden until dark, and then at his signal, we get up and follow closely behind him.

'The most important thing is to be absolutely quiet. Don't make a sound, boys,' he tells Jozef and Dovid, putting a finger to his lips.

Mama and Papa carry the boys, and keeping low we silently creep from alleyway to alleyway behind our guide. Suddenly he stops abruptly, motioning to us to stand still. From around the next corner I can make out the voices of a group of German soldiers chatting and joking with one another. Dovid begins to struggle in Mama's arms, his patience finally exhausted. Alerted, the Germans stop talking and listen for unusual sounds. Footsteps approach.

'We are done for,' I think to myself; but just as the soldier reaches the corner, a loud noise from one of the neighboring buildings startles a mangy cat perched above us. It gives an angry meow, jumps down and, carelessly scattering a pile of garbage, paws its way noisily towards the soldiers. Laughter is followed by retreating boots. Papa looks heavenward and mouths his gratitude. My heart is pumping wildly and for a moment I'm afraid I will never breathe normally again.

Once he is certain that the Germans have gone, Mr. Frenkel leads us on until we come to the rear entrance of a large building.

'My family's apartment is on the third floor,' he whispers.

'Take off your shoes so that your footfalls are muffled on the stairs.'

He ushers us inside, and I follow him on tiptoes up the winding staircase. He stops in front of an impressive, heavily carved wooden door, and gives a long knock, followed by three short ones, and another long one. After a moment, a woman slowly opens the door and Mr. Frenkel falls into her arms. Thankfully, his wife and daughter are safe, and they are relieved and delighted to be reunited.

Mrs. Frenkel welcomes us all into their home, which is shrouded in darkness. She apologizes, but explains that we mustn't risk drawing attention to ourselves from outside by turning on lights.

'We will get organized in the morning, but meanwhile let me give you some refreshment, although I don't have much to offer.'

After a drink and a quick wash, Mama and Papa draw us close to them, the little ones whining from fear and exhaustion. I too am exhausted from the past days' events and I drift off into a deep sleep.

Chapter 6

Przemyśl

Przemyśl is a busy city spanning two sides of the San River. Papa once visited the city and knows quite a lot about it. When I ask him why it's an important center, he explains that its geographical location, connecting the Carpathian Mountains with fertile lowlands, and its strategic position on the navigable waterway, account for Przemyśl's long and rich history, and its importance on Central European trade routes.

'It also has a thriving Jewish community,' he tells me. 'I think over a quarter of the city's population are Jews.'

The Frenkel's apartment building stands not far from the town center and the marketplace, on the east bank of the river. Their rooms cover half of the third floor, with windows both in the front and back. Their daughter, Magda is my age, and has her own large room, which I am to share with her. Mama and Papa have a room to share with the boys. Mr. Frenkel owns a cosmetics company on the opposite side of the river, and appears to be very successful. The apartment is well appointed, with soft carpets and rich drapes, beautiful pieces of furniture and decorative objects.

Mr. Frenkel explains to Papa that, with the arrival of the German army, he dismissed the housekeeper, informing her that the family was leaving town. In order to maintain the ruse that the apartment is unoccupied, we are instructed to be as quiet as possible, and not to stand at the windows for fear of being noticed. On the first morning, however, hoping to get a first impression of the town, I dare to peek gingerly out of one of the windows. The surrounding buildings are quite closely packed together, under the watchful eye of a regiment of church spires standing sentinel over the town, topped by golden crosses glinting in the sunlight.

Mrs. Frenkel is embarrassed by the inadequate meals she prepares for us.

'Since the Germans arrived,' she tells Mama, 'food is in short supply. At first, I dared to sneak out of the apartment to buy food for myself and Magda, but the soldiers have become more watchful.'

With our arrival, she is wary of rousing their suspicions by trying to buy enough supplies to feed all of us, and of drawing attention to the 'empty' apartment. Since Mr. Frenkel and Papa also have to keep out of sight, it's up to me and Magda to find food. I'm really excited by this new challenging role as provider of supplies and news from the outside.

Gathering news is a pretty straightforward task, but not a happy one. Returning from our first excursion, it falls to me to tell Mama and Papa the terrible news we overheard while queueing for bread.

'You remember those jeeps full of Nazi soldiers who passed us on the road to Sudova Vyshnya? Their orders were to murder all the town's Jews. The entire community has been annihilated, including our kind Hannah and her sons. I shudder to think what our fate would have been if we hadn't made our escape when we did.'

Mama gasps, and Papa merely shakes his head sadly from side to side.

Mama is worried about the risks of the responsibility

that has fallen on my shoulders, and has become sick. The wandering, anxiety and lack of proper nourishment have caused an ulcer, which has plagued her for years, to flare up. She won't admit it, but I know what's really bothering her. She is finding it unbearable being a 'guest' in the various lodgings where we have taken shelter. At home she was always the first to offer hospitality and succor to the needy, but she absolutely hates being on the receiving end.

Every day just before dawn Magda and I slip out of the apartment, locking the door's huge padlock behind us, and venture out into the streets, mingling with the other children, Jewish and gentile, looking for supplies. The queues at the bakeries for a loaf of bread are endless, and sometimes we have to stand in line for hours. Between us we have a little money and jewelry to exchange for food, and when we dare to wander out of the city we can sometimes buy milk and butter from the local farmers at an exorbitant price. All in all we are pretty good at finding food, and while it's not plentiful no one complains of being hungry. And Magda and I are getting a great education in subterfuge and stealth.

We usually spend the whole day away from the apartment, waiting to return just before curfew, when it's almost dark. We have mapped out a myriad of paths and alleyways, allowing us to alternate our route home and throw off anyone who attempts to follow us. However, our biggest challenge is getting inside the building without using the front entrance.

Aneta, the daughter of the building's janitor, is, to put it bluntly, a prostitute. Thanks to Erna, I know exactly what that means. Mama would be horrified if she knew about the whore, and about my knowledge of the profession. Every afternoon, Aneta leans invitingly against the entrance door of the building, with her skirt hitched up above her knees to show off her legs, and peddles her services to a long line of German soldiers. If she's willing to sell her own body, we are sure she would not hesitate to turn us in for a few zloty.

'But how can we avoid drawing attention to ourselves, alerting the soldiers, or giving Aneta or her father cause to check the apartment?' I asked Magda on our first outing, hoping she had a solution to the problem.

'We can reach our building by running along the rooftops of neighboring houses, jumping from one to the next, and then we can climb down to the rear entrance.'

I thought she was mad, and I was pretty terrified at first, but I actually quite enjoy the thrill of the danger. The risks are numerous, but we are up for the challenge. On two occasions we have almost been caught. Coming home one evening carrying particularly heavy parcels, I tripped on a loose roof tile. Magda grabbed my arm, helping me to regain my balance, but the shingle toppled noisily down to the street. We held our breath, waiting for a commotion to start, but lucky for us no one was passing beneath the building at the time. The second time it was Magda's turn to lose her footing. She began to slide slowly down the roof, scraping her knees and elbows. At the last minute she managed to get a grip on the frame of a dormer window. When our hearts had returned to their normal beat, she slowly slid herself on her bottom back up to the top.

One evening on our way home, Magda and I overhear an alarming rumor that's circulating around the neighborhood. The Germans are getting ready to leave our side of the river. Before they go they are planning to burn down the Old Synagogue, which is located just a few houses away from the apartment in which we're hiding. When we report the rumor to Mr. Frenkel, he sends us outside to keep watch, terrified that the fire might spread to our building, and he tells us to be ready to raise the alarm if it does. We climb back up to the roof and take up a position from where we have an unobscured view of the synagogue.

The rumor is true, and soon we are witness to raucous soldiers setting the synagogue alight. As the fire gathers strength, the heat causes the beautiful windows to explode, and rivers of colored molten glass flow to the ground like blood and tears, while tongues of fire reach up towards the sky, like hands in prayer. Through my tears, I'm horrified to see gentile children in the street whooping and laughing, and collecting pieces of broken glass as prized mementos of the occasion.

Just when we fear that the wind will blow the fire in our direction, the Germans have a change of heart and decide to douse the flames, in order to prevent them spreading. And then, all at once they are moving out, a parade of tanks, command cars, and motor bikes, followed by a column of troops, whose heavy boots echo on the cobbled street. In the ensuing quiet, the only sound is the hissing of the desecrated synagogue in its death throes. The air is filled with acrid smoke, ashes circulate in the wind, and the charred remains of the synagogue cower in humiliation.

Exhausted from our vigil, Magda and I return to the apartment and report to the family. The tragic sight of the burning building is etched in our memory, and Magda and I hold each other closely as we cry ourselves to sleep.

When we wake up the following morning it's already light outside. Papa comes to rouse us, announcing, 'The Germans have gone, the Russians have taken control.'

It seems that with the invasion of Poland by the German and Soviet armies, a pact between them has ruled that the San River is to become the German-Soviet border, effectively cutting the town in two. Mr. Frenkel's apartment is located on the east bank of the river, so that following the Germans' departure we find ourselves thrown into Russian hands.

Slowly, the Jews begin to come out of their hiding places, and go about their business. It's a relief to be able to come and go freely from the apartment, without having to jump over roofs or circumvent soldiers. The daily influx of new refugees looking for sanctuary seems endless. On the west side of the San, the German side, Jews have been ordered to leave within twenty four hours, and make their way across the railway bridge to the Russian side. Anyone caught on the German side after that will be shot.

Mr. Frenkel's cosmetics factory is located on the German side of the river, and he's desperate to save what he can from it. But he doesn't dare to attempt to cross over. Once again, Magda and I are called upon to use our wits to outsmart the soldiers. The first challenge is the Russian checkpoint at our end of the bridge. If we manage to successfully pass these guards and make it across the bridge, we will then be faced by German soldiers at the other end. On our return we will have to run the gauntlet again.

Terrified that the guards will notice us going backwards and forwards, we conjure up a plan to confuse them. I no longer possess changes of clothing, but Magda has a closet full of lovely dresses, skirts and sweaters. She also has numerous pairs of shoes and boots. Even if it wasn't wartime, and I wasn't reduced to one outfit, I would be green with envy. Each day we choose a different combination, accessorized by an assortment of hats and scarves, fooling the soldiers who fail to recognize that the same two girls are going back and forth across the bridge. It's a veritable fashion parade. We make several forays, each time smuggling small parcels from Mr. Frenkel's factory hidden under our coats. When we return to our side of the river Mr. Frenkel and Papa are waiting to relieve us of our burden. We carry out this ruse for several days until the bridge is finally closed, by which time we have succeeded in retrieving a fair amount of Mr. Frenkel's property.

My perilous adventures with Magda make me long for Erna, left behind in Tsanz to an uncertain fate. She would have relished the excitement of our subterfuge, disregarding any notions of danger, or the consequences of being caught. I savor the thought of relating to her how we tricked the German and Russian soldiers, but, at the same time, I worry so much about what has become of her and her family.

Chapter 7

Khodoriv

Several weeks have passed since we fled Tsanz and set out on our self-imposed exile, although it seems much longer. Papa has decided that we have been enough of a burden to our host in Przemyśl, and that it's time to move on. Our money is all but gone, and Papa needs to look for work.

'I have been asking around,' he tells us one day, 'and it seems that there is a defunct sugar factory not too far from here, in a small town called Khodoriv. If I can lay my hands on some sugar, I will be able to produce candies and sweets, even if the conditions are primitive.'

Since these items are a luxury, Papa expects that he will be able to sell them at a good profit.

Once again we pack up our meager possessions, and Magda is kind enough to let me choose a couple of dresses, a sweater, a pair of gloves and a warm scarf from her collection. Despite our brief friendship, a strong bond has been forged between us, and I'm sorry to say goodbye. Mama and Papa thank the Frenkels for their kindness and generosity, and, having wished each other 'good luck', we make our way to the train station.

When I was out and about with Magda, I passed this building several times, and I've been impressed by the grandeur of its exterior, but as we step inside, it is the interior that amazes me, its elegant beauty more suited to a stately home than a train station. The entrance hall is two stories high, with tall arched doorways at ground floor level, matched by tall arched windows above them. The room is lit by a leaded skylight in the center of the decorative ceiling, and by several magnificent chandeliers. Thank goodness the Germans weren't tempted to destroy this as well before they left town.

Papa buys our tickets and we board the train. The journey to Khodoriv is a short one, and soon we are approaching our destination. Papa points out of the carriage window to a large red brick building, with a tall chimney stack rising high above its roof.

'That must be the sugar refinery,' he says. 'I will go there once we are settled.'

As soon as we get out of the station, Papa goes in search of the first of the three esses –somewhere to live. Khodoriv is a small industrial town, and available accommodation is scarce. After many fruitless inquiries, he rents the only place which is vacant.

'Come along, children.' he invites us, 'Come and see your new home.'

'A shop?' Mama asks incredulously. 'How can we live in a shop?'

Papa is very unhappy with her snobbish reaction, and is quick to put her in her place.

'In Tsanz,' he reminds her, 'your parents live on the second floor above their shop. We will just have to make do with the ground floor.'

Never one to be deterred, Papa sets about converting the shop into an apartment. The space comprises two areas, a large open section in the front, and a small kitchen at the rear. Accepting help from local Jews, who are eager to welcome 'the poor refugees' and lend a hand, Papa furnishes the 'apartment' with beds, a table and chairs, and some dishes. The large front space serves as our living quarters, while the kitchen doubles as a place to prepare the family meals, and as a 'manufacturing plant' for Papa.

While the town itself is quite ugly and the houses rather drab, the synagogue is a wonderful surprise. The exterior of the old wooden building is very plain, but inside it's decorated with the most beautiful, richly-colored paintings. Not even one tiny space is left bare on the vividly painted, high arched ceiling, whose central feature is a circle of brightly colored signs of the Zodiac. A regal lion and a unicorn, standing opposite each other look as if they might be dancing; three cheeky rabbits chase each other head to fluffy tail in a circle; simple fish and sheep mingle with exotic monkeys, leopards and parrots. In the middle of the room stands the *bima*, the Rabbi's pulpit, surrounded by a balustrade of intricate metalwork; and on the wall facing Jerusalem in the East, six steps lead up to the ark which holds the Torah scrolls, elaborately carved and standing at least twenty feet high.

Once we are organized, Papa sets out to find out what he can about the sugar factory. He discovers that before the Soviet invasion of Poland, the Khodoriv sugar mill was the largest one in this region, which is now part of the Ukraine. However, with the onset of war its production and marketing almost ground to a halt, leaving unsold sacks in the factory's warehouse. The manager is happy to sell the sugar. Papa negotiates a good price for a plentiful supply, and he immediately sets to work making candies.

The aroma from the kitchen which wafts into the rest of the apartment is mouth-watering. When he has produced a small supply, Papa takes me on an exploratory tour of the town, to look for a suitable spot to set up his business.

'The railway station is definitely the busiest hub,' he decides, 'and I won't be hampered by competition there, as I would be if

I tried to set up shop in the marketplace.'

Every day, he opens his stall outside the station, and hawks his produce to travelers and passers-by. News soon spreads about his kiosk, which quickly proves to be a great success, as he had predicted. In no time at all, the enterprise begins to make a substantial profit.

Unfortunately, while we now have money, there is nothing to buy in Khodoriv, especially clothing, which we all need desperately.

'Lwow is the nearest large city,' says Papa. 'I'll go there and see what I can buy.'

The bad memories of our stop in Lwow are still fresh in my mind, and I don't want him to go back there.

'Papa, it's not safe. We were there only a few weeks ago, and were nearly killed in an air raid.'

'Nowhere is completely safe, Tanya'leh. But the Germans are no longer interested in Lwow, which is now under Russian control. Now, everyone, tell me what you need.'

Our many weeks on the road have left me with shoes which are torn and irreparable. My feet are not the same size as Magda's, otherwise I could have taken a pair from her. So, I'm delighted when Papa returns from his first shopping expedition, and presents me with brand new pair. They are very pretty, but sadly much too tight. I'm very grateful for the gesture and anxious not to hurt his feelings, so I pretend they are comfortable, and suffer the discomfort of pinched feet in silence. On his next trip, I am rewarded with a long, dark blue coat, which is soft and warming. Mama asks him to bring some fabric, from which she makes some curtains for our 'living room' and a table cloth. Not long ago in Tsanz, these would have been considered trivialities, but nowadays the most mundane items are hard- to-come-by luxuries.

Our neighbors are kind, but I fight against acknowledging my status, in their eyes, as an unfortunate refugee, or accepting their sympathy. In the main they speak Yiddish, a language I don't know well, or Russian which is also foreign to me, and I find their ways quite primitive. On the other hand, I know they mean well, and I don't want to end up being a snob like Mama, so I try to act as gracious and grateful as possible.

After the past few weeks eluding the Nazis, life seems to be returning to some sort of normalcy under the Russians. I discover that education is one of their top priorities, and that all the town's children are required to attend school. I'm keen to resume my education, make new friends, and relieve the boredom of staying at home and entertaining my little brothers. With these goals in mind, I approach my first day at school with enthusiastic anticipation.

However, almost immediately my enthusiasm is crushed. All the classes are taught in Ukrainian, Russian, or Yiddish. How will I be able to study or make friends if I can't understand or communicate? I feel like a complete outsider and terribly alone, and yearn for Erna and my classmates from Tsanz. There are two other refugees in my class, and not surprisingly we drift towards each other. We feel foreign in every way – our dress, our living conditions, and our lack of language.

I come home from school miserable and bad tempered. I'm short with my brothers, and unhelpful at home. I beg Papa to take us back to Tsanz, to my familiar world, my home, my possessions, my friends.

'Perhaps the Germans have left there already, Papa, and we are punishing ourselves for no reason.'

All my attempts to convince him are unsuccessful.

One evening he beckons me to come and sit with him.

'Tanya'leh,' he says, 'I have had news of life at home. I wanted to spare you the truth, but you are old enough to hear the facts and understand why we must stay away for now.'

He explains that the Germans have closed down all the Jewish institutions, and Jewish stores, including Grandfather's delicatessen, have been confiscated. Jews were being taken into forced labor.

'They are required to sew a Star of David armband on to their clothes, and are restricted in their movement around the town. For the time being,' he insists unhappily, 'there can be no going back'.

I continue to wallow in my misery until one day an unexpected visitor knocks at our door. The stranger introduces himself and says he has brought us news of Grandfather.

'Someone saw him making his way on foot to Tarnów. It was pouring with rain, and he was cold and wet because he wasn't wearing a coat.'

I gasp at the mention of the coat, which Grandfather had entrusted to my care, and which had burnt to a cinder on the bombed train at Sudova Vyshnya.

'He was crying because he thought you had all perished. Happily he reached Tarnów safely and was reunited with his wife and other members of your family.'

Papa thanks the visitor for taking the trouble to let us know, and immediately writes a letter to Grandfather telling him that we're safe, and updating him on our experiences since being parted from him in Bobowa.

Knowing that Grandfather is alive pulls me out of my depression, and I'm determined to make every effort possible to succeed at school and make him proud of me. I discover that some lessons are also taught in German, in which I and my two refugee friends are proficient. We are also the best at gym and drama, and these talents help to bridge the gap between us and the other children, who begin to accept and include us. I'm also picking up Ukrainian quite quickly, and my Yiddish is also improving.

One morning the school principal addresses the assembly.

'Children, pay close attention please. A gymnastics Olympiad is to be held in Kiev, one of the largest cities in the Ukraine. Each school will send a delegation of its most outstanding gymnasts to participate in the competition.'

There is a flurry of excitement as the principal announces that the school will hold its own competitive gymnastics display, in order to choose the team to represent us at the Olympiad. Children are divided into teams, and the race is on. My class's team includes me and my two German friends. How we practice and practice, trying to perfect our flick-flacks, twirls and splits! Our teacher is strict and exacting, barking instructions and criticisms, until she is satisfied with our performance. After weeks of training, the day of the competition finally arrives. My excitement is tempered by anxiety. What if I make a mistake and let the whole team down? What if one of the other teams is better than us? How we long to win!

As the competition progresses, team after team present their routines. It seems like our turn will never come, and then, all at once, we are on the floor. The music begins and we launch into our performance. I feel like I have wings; I am free as a butterfly, released from the dark cocoon of my homeless nightmare. I float with the music, engrossed in my exercises. In what seems like the blink of an eye the performance is over, and the spell is broken. As we leave the floor our teacher smiles; we have made her proud.

Now we have the nerve-wracking, nail-biting wait for the judges' decision. I fear my heart will burst when the principal announces that our team will be the one to represent the school at the Olympiad. There is much clapping and hugging. The principal congratulates us.

'You have made a wonderful effort. Keep it up and bring home the trophy from the Olympiad.'

I can't wait to hurry home and tell my parents about this exciting achievement. Feeling truly happy for the first time since leaving home, I burst into the apartment.

'We're going to Kiev. My team won the competition, and we're going to represent the school in Kiev. I'm so excited, and it's such an honor,' I shout, dancing around the room.

Papa cuts short my rejoicing. 'Tanya'leh, I'm sorry but there is a war waging outside. There will be no travelling to Kiev. The whole family is staying put here, together. Who knows what tomorrow may bring?'

By the look on Papa's face and the tone of his voice, I know that there is no point arguing. I am furious and heartbroken. Frustrated that I don't even have my own room to run to, my own door to slam, my own private domain to sit in while I rage and sulk, I crouch down in the furthest corner of the kitchen and sob quietly.

Crestfallen, I drag myself to school the following day, to tell my teacher that I won't be permitted to accompany the team to Kiev. She comes to our house to try to persuade Papa, but it's no use. His mind is made up, and that's that. That afternoon, I stand outside the school gates, kicking at stones to release my anger and frustration. Suddenly, a brightly-dressed gypsy woman crosses my path.

'Why so forlorn, young lady?' she asks. 'Would you like me to guess why, and tell you your fortune?'

'I have no money to pay for fortune-telling,' I reply, but she continues anyway.

Her rows of bangles jangle playfully at her wrist as she takes my hand in hers. Inspecting it closely she pronounces, 'You were born on a holy day, a day of fasting.'

My breath catches in my throat, and wide-eyed I confirm, 'That's true. I was born on Yom Kippur, the holiest of days.'

Her dark eyes look penetratingly into mine.

'Do not be sad, little one. Things will be bad for a time, but you will have good luck. You will have a full and happy life.'

Releasing my hand, she goes on her way. I'm feeling so miserable about not going to Kiev that I find it impossible to take her fortune-telling seriously, and I wave off her prediction.

Once again, Papa's worries turn out to be justified. Just two days after my team leaves for Kiev without me, there is a knock at the door late at night, and Papa opens it to a Russian soldier.

'Get dressed at once,' he orders. 'Take what possessions you can carry, and come with us.'

Unnerved, we gather together what we can, and stumbling out into the dark street, we join a stream of other families being herded towards the railway station, where a long freight train of cattle trucks awaits us.

Chapter 8

Heading East

For several weeks, Papa had been wrestling with a difficult dilemma. The Russian authorities offered refugees from the West two options: to stay in Russia and receive citizenship, or to return to German-annexed Poland. Papa weighed these two alternatives and reasoned, 'I am still young enough to serve in the army. If I accept help from the Russians they will surely conscript me, and the family will be left here all alone. If I declare that I wish to return to Poland, I am betting that they won't be able to repatriate us across the border, since the Germans will refuse to let us back in.'

After considerable deliberation and lengthy discussions with others in the same situation as ours, he reached the decision to reject the offer of citizenship, convinced that we would be able to live out the war under Russian protection but without obligations.

The Russian authorities, it seems, have other ideas. When we are assembled, together with many other refugees who made the same decision as Papa, the soldiers slide open the wagon doors, and we are pushed up and into the dirty wagons.

Affixed horizontally to three sides is a large, wide shelf, which divides the wagon into two levels. Some families are allocated places below the shelf, while others occupy the upper level. My family is squeezed with at least fifty other people into the upper section of our wagon, and we juggle for space for ourselves and our belongings.

One of the soldiers points to a hole in the middle of the floor, and tells us that it is to serve as our toilet. As soon as the wagon is full to capacity, the door is heaved shut and locked from the outside, and the train begins to move slowly out of the station.

In this nightmarish situation, we find ourselves cramped in the closest of quarters with a large number of unfamiliar people; children, teenagers, adults and the very old, mostly Jews. Everyone sits in stunned silence, trying to digest this turn of events. Terrified, my brothers Jozef and Dovid huddle closely into Mama, who tries to encourage them with familiar Yiddish and Polish nursery rhymes and lullabies. Jozef's favorite is *Wlazł kotek na płotek* (a cat sat on the fence). When Mama sings *Patshe, patshe kikhelekh* (clap, clap little cookies), little Dovid happily joins in, enthusiastically clapping his hands. Gradually, several other mothers and small children sing along.

It would take much more than *Rozhinkes mit Mandlen* (Raisins and Almonds), however, to sweeten my mood or boost my morale. I'm still smarting from my missed opportunity in Kiev, and this current humiliation is the last straw. Quite naturally and unfairly, I direct my misplaced anger at Papa, deeming everything his fault.

I turn my back on the family and focus my attention on the passing countryside. Through a small window in the wagon's side I can make out the names of stations through which the train passes, and it soon becomes very clear that we are heading east towards the Russian border. The journey is excruciatingly slow. Stopping and starting, stopping and starting. The wagon remains firmly closed, and the smells within it quickly become very unpleasant.

Someone fashions a sheet into an improvised screen around the toilet hole, and while this affords some privacy, shielding users from the eyes of their fellow travelers, the sounds and odors can't be muffled. Balancing steadily over the hole is nigh on impossible when the train is in motion, especially for the female passengers. Sitting down or leaning on one's hands is unthinkable, due to other passengers missing the target. There is no water for drinking let alone for washing hands. So whenever the train slows to a standstill there is a rush for the 'facilities', with much pushing and shoving. If the train stops at a station we stretch out our arms through the small window to beg for water. Sometimes people take pity on us and, in the spirit of camaraderie, the water they proffer is shared fairly among all the wagon's inmates.

Once a day, guards open the wagon doors and dish out a thin soup, our only sustenance apart from the meager provisions Mama has brought with us, which are soon depleted. It tastes disgusting and is in no way nourishing, but Mama insists we eat up our entire ration, reasoning that 'something, however unappetizing, is better than nothing.'

After a few days, the crowded conditions, the odors and the filth make me start to imagine all sorts of creepy-crawlies roaming around my body. One afternoon I doze and dream I am back in Tsanz. Running through *Venice* is a little stream which is especially favored by us children. The nearside bank is higher than the opposite side, and a popular competitive game involves taking turns to jump across from the lower bank up to the higher one. More often than not some unsuccessful contestant would fall in. The shallow water is refreshingly cool, but, unfortunately, also plays host to uninvited participants in our frivolities. The unlucky ones amongst us would emerge from the water accompanied by loathsome leeches, which were very unpleasant to remove.

I awake from my dream to find my arms covered in scratches, where I have tried to pick off the imaginary creatures in my sleep.

To my dismay, it turns out that infestation is not a mere

figment of my imagination. Several children have begun to scratch their heads and complain of itching. I keep my hair tightly braided, but this is not enough in such close confines to protect me. After about a week into the journey my spirit breaks. I can see lice crawling in my long dark braids. Horrified, I seize a pair of scissors from the bag of an old lady sitting quite near to me, and hack off my hair before Mama realizes what I am doing and tries to stop me.

'Tanya'leh,' she screams, as she sees me hurl my butchered hair out of the window.

'What have you done?'

I curl myself up into a tight ball, and let myself descend into the depths of despair and despondency. I stop eating the little there is. Sleeping most of the time, I escape from reality into my dreams and memories.

The journey drags on, and, as is to be expected in such close quarters, people start to become bad-tempered with each other, complaining about snoring, and poking, and passing gas. The weather outside is getting colder and colder, and while the fresh air coming in through the window brings some relief from the stale, rank air inside the wagon, we now have to huddle even closer together to keep warm. More than anything, I long for some privacy and personal space.

Almost three weeks after leaving Khodoriv, the train finally arrives at its destination. The wagon doors are unlocked, and we are instructed to get down. There is an audible sigh of relief as, one by one, families climb down and stretch their legs, shaking off the confines of the past weeks like a dog drying its wet fur after a dip in the sea. Children are running around excitedly in the field next to the railway tracks, shouting and laughing. Suddenly the heavens open up, and torrential rain begins to fall. We hastily gather up our belongings and run for cover under a nearby bridge. Mama grimaces and grumbles, 'Look at us. We have turned into homeless gypsies, living under a bridge.'

I don't care; I quite like the idea of being an unencumbered gypsy, free as a bird to roam in the open air, wherever my fancy takes me. I recall the Romany woman who told my fortune outside the schoolyard not so long ago, praying that my luck is about to change as she predicted.

The train's destination, however, is not ours. Papa has no idea where we are, and the guards don't enlighten us. They point in the direction of some moored boats.

'Tomorrow you will continue your journey by river.'

As soon as the rain eases, we are marshalled into a dank warehouse for the night, the only source of fleeting warmth being the daily ration of thin soup, dished out before the doors are closed on us.

The following morning, stiff and shivering, we board the boats, which are, in fact, open river barges. These large, wooden flat-bottomed contraptions, traditionally used to ship cargoes of coal, sand, or crushed stones, have been reassigned to become people transporters. Once again, we are crammed together like sardines, but now, instead of the claustrophobic, hot interior of the cattle trucks, we are exposed to the elements.

Although the river is fairly calm, many passengers, including Mama, can't abide the rolling movement of the barge, and are miserably seasick. Those of us who are not affected by the motion, suffer anyway from the retching of those next to us. There is no space to distance ourselves from the sound and smell of their gagging. After a number of days, we are finally put ashore. We stumble gratefully onto dry land, but our relief that the voyage is over is short-lived.

As soon as the barges have deposited their human load, we are herded into trucks, which take us overland to a second river.

'This is the Lena River.' a guard tells us.

'Tomorrow,' he continues, pointing to another fleet of barges lying in wait, 'you will to take the final leg of your journey.'

We are still unsure of where precisely we are, until one of the passengers bemoans, 'We are in Siberia. All is lost.'

Siberia? What and where is Siberia, I wonder. Are we still in Russia? The geography we learned in school was very general. I know where most of the countries of Europe are in relation to Poland. We learned a little about Marco Polo's travels to the Kublai Khan in China, and Columbus's discovery of the Americas, but I've never heard of a place called Siberia.

We are weak from hunger and travel sickness. Mama is listless, and it's left to me to occupy the boys, whose initial childish excitement of boats and trucks has dissipated. The barges sail for many days, taking us deeper and deeper into the desolate wilderness, and I'm gripped by a fear of the unknown fate that awaits us.

Chapter 9

The Middle of Nowhere,
Autumn 1940

'This is your new home,' says the guard, pointing towards a motley array of sad-looking log cabins clustered at the river's edge. The primitive huts are constructed from roughhewn logs piled one on top of the other, cemented together by mud and moss, which insulate the cracks between them.

And so begins our exile. Although we have been refugees for over a year, I've clung to my belief that we would soon return home to Nowy Sącz. After all, our temporary shelter until now has been found in towns and villages within Poland, or in close proximity to its border, from where a short train ride would take us home once the war was over. Siberia is a different story. We are miles and miles from civilization, thrown haplessly together with 'enemies of Russia', be they Jews, Poles, Russians, capitalists, priests, political agitators, dissidents, or just unlucky individuals, left to be forgotten in a vast expanse of nothingness, until forced labor, hunger and cold crushes our spirit and defeats our bodies. This is true exile bereft of hope or future.

We are ushered into 'our' hut, together with two other families. The small entrance area is dominated by a large, heavy stove, so I assume it is probably the kitchen. Beyond this are two more tiny rooms. I take a look around in dismay. Each of the cramped spaces is furnished with one wide wooden bench, which I realize is to serve as a bed for the entire family. We are allotted the kitchen, and the other families take the two rear rooms. Papa, who constantly tries to lift our spirits, laughingly notes our good fortune.

'We are nearest to the door, so it will be easier to reach the outhouse, and in the winter we will light the stove and enjoy its warmth.'

Mama and Papa get us organized as much as is possible, and we settle down for the night. For now, it seems, we will have to make do with the warmth from each other's bodies as we sleep side by side. There are no real blankets, and we cover ourselves with coats and whatever other rags we can find. I remember Grandfather's thick warm coat that he entrusted to me, and choking tears rise in my throat, for the loss of the coat and of his presence, both of which would have made our situation a bit more bearable.

The true Siberian winter, of which we have been warned, has not yet begun, but I am already chilled to the bone, and I can't imagine how it will be possible to survive the impending bitter coldness. At least we don't have to share a room with another family, but it soon becomes apparent that our quarters will be a thoroughfare, traversed by the other tenants, as they come and go to work, or need the outhouse.

The morning after our arrival all the newcomers congregate outside. The veteran prisoners explain that we are located deep inside northern Siberia, next to Bodaybo, a gold mining settlement in the Irkutsk district, about fifteen hundred kilometers north of the border with Mongolia. Some of them have lived in exile here for many years. However, many others didn't survive the back-breaking work and harsh conditions.

'You have been allocated the huts of those who succumbed,' the locals grimly inform us.

If this isn't frightening enough, the first order of the day makes me physically shudder.

'You see that white hill over there behind the settlement?' a guard says pointing to a spot in the distance. 'That will be your cemetery, where many of you are likely to end up. Go up there now and begin digging graves, because once the winter sets in it will be impossible to shift the frozen earth, and a lack of graves will necessitate the storage of bodies until the spring thaw.'

This speech is delivered with no hint of sarcastic humor or emotion; it is merely a statement of fact. We are also warned that, with winter just around the corner, if we don't collect and store sufficient wood we will have no heat and we'll freeze to death.

I turn to Papa. 'What do we know of digging graves and collecting wood?'

Mama wears an expression of horror on her face, as she clutches Dovid and Jozef to her side. Papa tells her to stay in the hut, and signals to me to accompany him up to the 'hill of death', as I name it.

'Don't worry, Papa,' I assure him bravely. 'I will pull my weight and help you get the job done.'

This show of bravado is soon snuffed out, as I struggle to wield the heavy shovel while attempting to blot out the implications of this macabre task.

After we have done our fair share of digging, we are taken under the wing of a couple of locals, who show us where to gather wood, and how to pile and store it in such a way that it will survive the elements and last through the coldest months.

By the end of the day, I am exhausted and dejected. Papa sits down with me, and taking my sore hands in his, explains that the best way to survive is to make a game out of it.

'Just think, Tanya'leh. Today, you and I have learned two new skills – grave digging and wood collecting. How useful to have this new knowledge, which you never dreamed to possess. Take the opportunity to learn as much as you can in good humor, since you never know when it might be an asset.'

I wonder how Papa became so wise and of such strong spirit, and his attitude deepens the love and respect I already have for him. I decide that I will try to do my best, to make him proud of me, and give him one less reason for worry.

Mama must also learn new skills if we're not going to starve to death. Never was the adage *'Necessity is the mother of invention'* truer than in Siberia. The locals teach her about the indigenous vegetation and weeds, those which are poisonous and others which are edible, and she begins to concoct soups out of whatever is to hand. On the rarest of occasions we manage to get a potato, the ultimate luxury, which we share between us. But gnawing hunger is my constant companion.

Bread is rationed at one kilo per family per day. At first this sounded like a generous amount, but the bread is made by mixing a large proportion of water with coarse flour, resulting in a solid lump of dough, which is baked in small tins. By the end of the process one kilo is a very small piece indeed. Mama wakes me before dawn each morning, and sends me to wait in the long line to receive our daily ration. On the first day, I rush home with the warm 'loaf', fueled by the anticipation of food in my stomach, but when I get there Mama takes the bread and sets it aside.

'It's not healthy to eat the bread while it is still hot. It will give us stomach problems.' she cautions.

Once it has cooled, Mama divides it into equal portions for each of us, allocating half the quantity for breakfast, while keeping the rest for the evening.

The settlement is not enclosed by wire fencing; there are no guard towers or vicious dogs. There is no need, since there is nowhere to run. We are bordered by the river on one side and surrounded by *taiga* – the *land of the little sticks* in Mongolian – the collective name for the northern forests of Russia, dominated by coniferous larches, spruces and pines. Unlike the forests of Szczwanica, which beckoned me happily every summer, and wrapped me in a familiar blanket of scents and sounds, the taiga seems strange, formidable and unwelcoming.

Everyone is required to work. We are told, 'You will live by the basic tenet of socialism: *He who does not work, does not eat.*'

Papa joins the other men and older boys, who become laborers for the Russian logging industry, swinging axes and chopping down the trees. Women and children are assigned the less physical task of gathering up the thin branches and twigs, and of collecting woodland berries. On the first day, I stand in line with the others to receive a large pail, which I am required to fill by the evening. The berries can be used for bartering at the local 'store', in exchange for a piece of salted fish or, perhaps, a few potatoes. Through lack of choice we learn to stomach the berries, which are very sour, and cause a variety of digestive problems, until our bodies become accustomed to their bitterness and acidity.

My new life takes on a kind of monotonous regularity. The day begins with the bread line, followed by berry-picking or twig-gathering, and later I help Mama with my brothers, keeping them occupied by telling them stories, just as I did on our summer vacations.

We have all been solemnly cautioned never to venture alone into the taiga, or wander far from the settlement, since it's easy to get lost or fall prey to bears and other wild animals.

'You never know who or what might step out of the taiga uninvited,' we are warned.

This warning provides me with a wellspring of material for making up frightening tales with which to entertain the boys. However, one day my fertile imagination becomes a frightening reality.

The older girls are sometimes sent further into the woods to gather twigs. We go out in groups of ten and focus our search in the hills above the settlement. On this particular day my group ventures a little farther than usual and, as darkness falls, we can't seem to find our path and become unsure of our way home.

'If we walk in the direction of the river and the rising moon we will reach the settlement,' reasons our group leader.

So we listen carefully and follow the distant sound of rushing water. It's now pitch dark and a swirling mist has descended, hovering between the trees, disorienting us and hampering our progress. After some time we realize that we're completely lost. After several more minutes have passed, we suddenly stumble upon a wide asphalt road.

'What on earth?' we ask each other, stunned by this incongruous sight, so out of place in the uninhabited forest.

'Where can this road possibly lead?'

We are terrified that we have wandered so far we'll never find our way back to the camp.

In an attempt to calm the mood, as I do with my brothers, I begin to concoct a fairy tale.

'Perhaps,' I suggest to my companions, 'we have entered a magical world. If we follow the road we will surely come upon an enchanted castle.'

For a bunch of children trying to survive a harsh life in a godforsaken wilderness, this suggestion is the ultimate fantasy, superseding caution and fear, and triumphing over plausibility. We begin to run excitably along the road, but after a minute or two we pull up sharply, eyes and mouths wide open, breath held. I was the one to conjure up the fantasy, but no one is more amazed than me to make out the dark silhouette of a castle in the distance, its majestic towers dominating the surrounding forest.

'Is this a mirage? Am I dreaming?' I wonder.

Step after nervous step, we continue cautiously until we reach the gates, but instead of a moat and portcullis we find a wire fence, look-out towers, and barracks. We shout and call out, but there is not a single soul inside, just an eerie silence and a haunted, spooky atmosphere. Petrified, we turn around and run as fast as we can, as if running from death itself.

Fearing all is lost as we run blindly along the road, we suddenly make out distant voices calling our names. A search party has come from the settlement to find us. We shout back as loudly as we can, 'over here, over here', until we see them in front of us.

Falling into our parents' arms, we recount excitedly what we have discovered, certain that no one is going to believe our story. The locals are amazed. They explain that our 'castle' was a former prison camp – *Bodaybo Ispravitelno-trudovoi Lage* – whose inmates had built the asphalt road '*that leads to nowhere*'. They all died from hard labor and starvation, and the prison was closed. Everyone had heard the rumor of the camp's existence, but no one knew its precise location in the forest; which is why they are so astonished by our discovery.

I'm deeply shaken by this experience, by the meshing of my fabrications with reality, the palpability of a ghostly presence more frightening than if I had met one of the taiga's notorious wild creatures. That night, and the nights that follow, I am plagued by nightmares, in which I picture the poor prisoners laboring to construct a purposeless road until they collapse. In the light of day, I can't help but wonder and fear that this is to be our fate as well.

One day, out of the blue, an incoming barge delivers some packages, and much to my amazement one of them is addressed to my family. It's from Grandfather. Papa explains that when we arrived at the settlement he sent a letter in the hope that it would reach our family in Poland, and incredibly it had. I don't know what thrills me more: what the package contains or the knowledge that Grandfather is still alive. Mama spreads out the contents and my heart begins to thump as my eyes recognize a pair of blue pants, stirring a strong memory from my last winter in Tsanz, which now seems like a lifetime ago.

In winter, the hill that leads towards the center of Tsanz is covered in a generous layer of snow, and it serves as our toboggan run. Townsfolk of all ages gather with their sleds at the top of 'Toboggan Hill' and race each other down. The ride starts out slow but quickly builds to a thrilling pace, accompanied by a cacophony of laughs and screams of both excitement and fear. I had a large sled on which I could take two or three companions, and the full complement propelled the sled even faster.

At the beginning of the last winter season, the year before the outbreak of war, Mama presented me with a beautiful new set of warm pants and matching top in a rich shade of royal blue. I couldn't wait to show them off to my friends, and, despite Mama's misgivings, I decided to wear them for the toboggan run. When I arrived at the top of the hill with my sled, I was delighted to be greeted with compliments and expressions of admiration for my new outfit.

Three of my friends seated themselves behind me on my sled, and off we went on our downhill race. A horse-drawn wagon, which conveyed ice taken from the frozen river and the lakes in *Venice* to storage warehouses in town, quite often stood at the foot of the hill. On this particular day, as we raced down towards the bottom of the hill, another sled spun off course and rammed into mine, hurtling us into the horses' hooves and the wagon's wheels. My friends and I were badly bruised and scratched. I had to be carried home, but the physical pain was nothing compared to the anguish I felt when I saw the gaping tear in my beautiful new pants, and saw the '*I told you so*' look on Mama's face.

Returning from my reverie to the present, I retrieve the pants and see that the tear has been neatly repaired, probably by one of my aunts. I finger the stitches, silently praying that whoever did the work is still safe and well, and that we will be reunited soon. To my delight the pants' disfigurement means that I can keep them. Everything else that can be exchanged for food will gradually disappear, but imperfect pants have little trade value.

The greatest treasure in the package, however, turns out to be a bottle of oil. We children are unimpressed, but when we see how Mama's face lights up we understand that there must be some hidden importance.

'This little bottle of oil will be our very own Chanukah Miracle,' she announces.

Although I'm pretty sure that it's not yet Chanukah, since the Jewish Festival of Lights falls in December, and the darkest days of winter have not yet arrived, I'm happy to listen to her recalling the two thousand year old story of the small jug of oil, retrieved from the desecrated Jewish Temple in Jerusalem. The boys are captivated as she retells the events.

'During the time of the Second Temple, the Holy Land was ruled by cruel Greeks. They robbed the Jews of their property, and set up idols in the holy Temple. No one could stand up against this powerful, brutal enemy, until a few courageous Jews called the Maccabees outwitted and defeated them. When the Maccabees entered the Temple, they found one solitary small jug of oil which had not been desecrated. They used it to light the Menorah candelabra, in order to rededicate the Temple. The quantity of oil was only enough for one day, but by a divine miracle it illuminated the Temple for eight whole days.'

In my mind's eye I can picture our silver Menorah at home. During the year it occupied pride of place on the sideboard in our dining room, but now it was hidden away from the Nazis in our basement. Every Chanukah, Mama would polish it until it shone brightly, and place it in front of the window of the apartment, where we, and passers-by in the street, could watch the candles burning brightly.

Now, coaxing Mama and the boys to join in, I begin to sing some of my favorite Chanukah songs; *Dreidel spin, spin, spin; Oh Chanukah, Oh Chanukah, A holiday, a lovely one*. We laugh and dance around, but then my mood turns somber.

'What I wouldn't give for some crispy *latkes* and sweet doughnuts,' I say to Mama, although I expect my stomach, now perpetually empty, would rebel against these traditional Chanukah foods, fried in oil to commemorate the miracle.

Mama uses the oil sparingly – a drop on a piece of bread or in a soup, to add extra nourishment and taste – and, miraculously, the bottle lasts for three months. The arrival of the package has brought a little light to the darkness of my existence, now made more bearable by the anticipation of future parcels, which I'm sure will follow. I don't realize that once winter comes and the river freezes over, there will be no communication, in or out, from our world. We will be completely cut off and isolated, and then despair will settle on my shoulders like a heavy cloak.

Chapter 10

Until Hell Freezes Over...

Winter has hit us like a hard slap in the face. The air is cold enough to make breathing an effort, and it feels like ice as it scrapes the back of my throat and brings tears to my eyes. My cheeks tingle with pain and my tears turn to frozen globules on my lashes. And I had thought that winters in Tsanz were harsh! I can recall days at home when snow storms battered my body as I walked to and from school, halting my progress and forcing me to take sanctuary next to a wall or in a doorway. Covering my face with my beret, I would turn away from the wind, crying with frustration and helplessness as I fought against its strength. If Mama saw me from the window of our apartment as I struggled to reach home, she would immediately come to my rescue. But such days in Tsanz were the exception rather than the rule.

Here in Siberia the wind is dry with only a few flurries of snow, but it is fiercer and more relentless and cruel than anything I have experienced in the past. Our crudely built cabin is no match for the wind's force, which rattles the windows and spreads a layer of ice on the interior walls. We children have been warned not to touch the windows, for fear that our skin will stick to the icy glass.

The kitchen stove burns round the clock, making our room the warmest in the cabin, but every time someone enters or goes out a blast of Arctic air sweeps through and spreads its chill. In order to benefit from the stove's heat, our house-mates leave the doors to their rooms open, compromising what little privacy we have. In the night, the wind's howling competes with that of the wolves in the forest. At first it sent chills up my spine, but I have become accustomed to its melancholic wail, and now I allow it to croon me to sleep.

Winter is accompanied by disease and death. The graves we dug upon our arrival are now occupied, as predicted, and the sheds are filled with homeless corpses waiting for burial after the thaw. First the children and the elderly succumb, those who have no reserves to fight off infection. Scurvy is rife, as there are no sources of Vitamin C. I remember the sailors I learned about in school, and how explorers such as Vasco de Gama discovered the curative effects of citrus fruit, saving their crews from this fatal affliction. I have to watch in horror as one of my new friends, Sarah, gradually transforms from a vivacious young girl into an old crone, as her lovely blond hair becomes brittle and falls out, and her gums swell and expel her teeth.

Papa has also been affected. He's been starving himself in order to give the boys a little extra food, and as a result he's developed night blindness. As it's almost dark most of the day and he can't see properly, he's lost his job, and has been reassigned to night duty guarding the tractor in the forest. He sleeps during the day and guards the tractor at night. Apparently, eyesight is not a requirement for this task. His job is to make sure the stove in the shed housing the tractor stays fired up, so that the engine doesn't freeze overnight. Since he can't see, he has to manage by feeling his way around, and quite often he comes home with a burn or two. It reminds me of his accidents making candy in the factory at home. I'm frightened for him because of his proximity to the wild forest animals, but he never complains or acts afraid.

Much to my amazement, the Russian emphasis on the importance of education holds true even in Siberia. Despite the bitter cold, children who are well enough to attend must go to school, in keeping with the government directive. The school is housed in a grey building, remarkable only by the fact that it's built of concrete and not of wood, and is located at the far end of the settlement. I estimate that it's about a half hour's walk, and I am dumbfounded as to how I'm expected to trek there without proper footwear, or keep warm without suitable clothes.

The work we do is remunerated in the currency of points, which are exchangeable for goods at the local market. Mama says that we can use them to purchase boots and coats. When we arrive at the market, I look around excitedly for the wonderful boots I am about to acquire, but all I can see are odd-looking slippers, which appear to have been crafted from pieces of rough blanket sewn rudely together and lined with raw wool. When I turn to Mama I'm surprised to see that she is haggling with the vendor for a pair of these slippers. I pull at her sleeve to get her attention.

'Not those, Mama. You don't seriously believe that they will survive the long walk to school and back, do you? They have no proper soles and will let in the rain. Please look for something sturdier.'

The vendor looks insulted by my outburst, but patiently explains that since the climate is mostly dry, these boots are not required to be waterproof, and that the felt from which they are fashioned is very resilient. I remain unconvinced.

Sensing my disappointment, Mama whispers that our points will only cover the cost of this type of 'boots', and that I will have to make do. The vendor, anxious to make the sale, asks me, 'Child, have you not noticed that these are the preferred footwear of all the locals?'

'But their boots are brightly colored with festive embroidery, not the dismal dun color of those in Mama's hand.' I complain.

I resign myself to the inevitable, but my disappointment evaporates as soon as I try them on. My feet are immediately engulfed by a warming softness, which spreads through the rest of my body. The coats we purchase are similarly crafted from heavy blanket-like material, which envelopes our bodies cozily, to insulate us from the cold wind, and preserve our body heat.

School represents a sort of normalcy in my life, rooted in a proper schedule and curriculum appropriate for my age, so I greet the opportunity with enthusiasm. This is summarily extinguished on the first day. My teacher is a huge, bulky-framed Tatar with a bulbous, pock-marked face, whose most prominent features are slanting Asiatic eyes and a nasty sneer. His tone is belligerent, and he bears undisguised malice towards the whole world, especially to Jews. His opening address to the class is: 'You will live here until you die here. Do not entertain any notions of freedom, of a future, or of control over your own destinies.'

His words are meant to be nullifying, and that is exactly their effect.

At the end of the first day, I walk dejectedly into our hut. Registering the expression on my face, Papa inquires, 'What is troubling you, Tanya'leh?'

'What is the point of going to school and studying, when there is no future in it?' I ask, having recounted my teacher's words.

Papa takes hold of my hand.

'An important philosopher once said that knowledge is power. Tanya'leh, education is the passport to your future. It will empower you to make choices and follow your dreams. No one can predict the future, least of all an ugly Tatar bully. Did we ever imagine living away from Tsanz in this desolate place? Do not give up hope. I promise you we will be rescued from our exile, and you will go to university in Eretz Israel. So you must keep up your studies.'

With Papa's encouragement I do my best to concentrate on my lessons, but there is no joy or stimulation in the classroom, and Mr. Tatar continues to torment us.

The long hours of winter darkness, the icy cold, and the lack of proper food gradually begin to deplete my strength, and finally take their toll. I fall sick with anemia. I am dizzy and listless, without enough energy to even lift my head off my bed. The settlement doctor is called, and after he examines me I hear him tell Mama and Papa that there is nothing to be done.

'Your daughter needs drugs which we do not have,' he apologizes.

Desperate, Mama goes in search of anyone who can help me. One of the locals directs her to a Catholic priest, a healer. Mama brings him to the cabin, and having looked at me, he announces, 'She needs iron, and the only source is in the forest. I will show you which plants and berries to gather, but you will have to feed them to her by force because they are very bitter.'

He was not exaggerating. Soon my mouth and tongue are burning from the unpalatable herbal medicine. The mixture makes me retch at first, but I want to get better and, understanding that I have no choice, I grit my teeth and endure it.

Gradually my strength begins to return. Friends from school come by to cheer me up, to tell me about the lessons I'm missing, and to complain about Mr. Tatar. One day, however, they rush into the cabin flushed with excitement.

'Tanya, you have to get well and come back to school. We have a new teacher. He's really nice and lets us dance and sing. He says that whoever does well in school will be able to leave here and go to Moscow or Leningrad to study.'

I don't believe a word of this for one minute. What sort of benevolent teacher would come all the way to Siberia to teach refugees and pariahs? I expect that they are just trying to get me back to school by any means, and I appreciate their efforts, even if their methods of persuasion include bending the truth.

Two weeks pass and I feel that I have revived enough to return to class. I'm happy to see the relief on my parents' faces when I announce that I am ready to go. I take the walk slowly to conserve my energy, so I'm the last to arrive in class. Entering the room, I immediately sense a change in the atmosphere, just like my friends described. I look towards the front of the class, and there stands the new teacher.

Suddenly the room is spinning, my legs feel weak, and my heart thumps wildly, threatening to burst from my chest. Collapsing into the nearest chair, I am swamped with the concerned attention of my friends, who worry that the long walk has been too much for me. I allow them to believe this rather than have them discover the real reason. As the teacher hurries anxiously towards me I avert my eyes, feeling the color rising in my cheeks, and my pulse begin to race again.

'Alright, class,' he says in a rich and resonant voice. 'Give your classmate some room.'

'You must be Tanya. Welcome back to school. I hope the effort to get here hasn't tired you too much.'

I hardly trust my own voice to answer, uncomfortable under his solicitous scrutiny. Trying to avoid eye contact I stammer nervously, 'I'm fine, thank you. Please don't worry,' silently willing him to return to the front of the classroom.

As he walks away, I try to calm the unfamiliar sensations coursing through my body, praying that he hasn't recognized the true source of my discomposure.

Chapter 11

Mikhail

The teacher's name is Mikhail. He is of average height and build, and his handsome face is framed by thick, dark, wavy hair, which contrasts compellingly with his piercing blue eyes. His voice is soft and full of concern as he asks if I'm alright, and his smile completely unbalances me. In one breath I am transformed into the heroine of one of Erna's romance novels. Mikhail is my hero, a knight in shining armor to my damsel in distress, Prince Charming to my Cinderella. I am instantly infatuated, helpless to resist the force of his attraction.

Mama notices that I have begun to take special care with my appearance. My hair has recovered from the brutal hacking aboard the railway train, and has grown back almost to its full length. I gasp from the shock of the icy water as I wash and brush it till it shines, adding a touch of pine oil from the forest. Much to my amazement, one morning soon after our arrival, Mama and I discovered a small patch of Lily-of-the-Valley among the trees. Before winter set in, Mama used to gather these and some other wild blooms to breathe a little life into our cabin. I pressed some of them, and now I rub the semi-dried flowers between my fingers and pat their perfume behind my ears.

Back home, as well as romance novels, Erna and I used to read Mama's women's magazine. Recalling several expert tips, I pinch my cheeks and bite my lips to give them color, as a substitute for

Szach's lipsticks, which advertised the promise of '*lips made for a kiss*'. When Mama comments on my new rituals, I offer her the explanation that behaving like a normal teenage girl helps me to survive the misery of our dislocation, and gives me hope of a return to life as it once was. She accepts this without further question, happy that I'm starting to take pride in my appearance. I will not share the real reason with anyone.

My friends have not bent the truth, and Mikhail does, indeed, encourage singing and dancing, creating a positive and enjoyable study environment. His mantra '*Anything is possible*' lifts our spirits and gives us hope. Mr. Slant-eyes Tatar has taken an instant dislike to him, behaving with outright hostility, not relinquishing any opportunity to offer snide remarks and undermine his efforts.

Mikhail treats me no differently to my classmates, and yet I sense an invisible bond drawing us together. The Siberian wilderness is the perfect setting for a novella, in which we are the principal characters; two desperate spirits, stagnating in the hellish waters of our lonely exile. In my mind, it's natural that we would drift towards each other, clinging to the illusion that the solace we would find in each other would ease our hopelessness.

I long to create opportunities to be alone with him outside of class, but the extreme cold does not allow for loitering or fabricated errands, and most of my time out of school is spent in the cabin with Mama and the boys.

At the end of my first week back at school, Papa decides that I'm well enough to take on a new chore. While I was sick my brother Jozef stood in line every morning for our bread ration. He is very proud of this new responsibility, and has no intention of relinquishing it. Relieved of this duty, I'm free to share the burden of fetching water from the frozen river. Every morning large holes are carved out of the two-meter thick ice, and buckets or other containers are lowered into the water and hauled back up when full. Some of the more proficient locals even manage to catch the odd fish. Fresh holes must be cut daily, since they freeze over again during the night.

On the first morning of my new assignment I join the crowd gathered at the river, and here, finally, I bump into Mikhail on neutral ground. He notices me from a distance, and hurries over to offer assistance. I'm aroused by his closeness, and when our hands brush briefly as he passes me my bucket of water I feel a frisson of electricity, even though our flesh is separated by layers of gloves.

Somehow, I manage to pluck up the courage to initiate a conversation, by telling him how much we all enjoy his lessons.

'I'm happy to hear that, Tanya, and I am particularly impressed by your diligence and enthusiasm for study.'

'Knowledge is power,' I reply, echoing Papa's words in the hope of impressing Mikhail. He raises an eyebrow in surprise.

'So, you are a philosopher as well as a lovely young lady.'

I blush at this unsolicited compliment, praying that my inner turmoil is not apparent on my face.

'I do love to read, and I miss my books terribly.'

Boldly, I suggest that perhaps he has some reading material which might interest me.

'Perhaps.' he replies, thoughtfully.

'Don't be late for class,' he adds, as he heads off in the direction of school, breaking the magical spell of our short-lived intimacy.

A few days later, Mikhail asks me to stay behind after class.

'I think you may enjoy this,' he says handing me a book.

'When you've finished reading, perhaps we can discuss it.'

Expecting some dog-eared classic, I'm surprised to see a brand new volume whose pages have not been turned by many readers.

'I understand that you enjoy tales of fantasy. But read carefully, because there is much to learn by searching for deeper meanings between the lines.'

The book is entitled *The Wizard of the Emerald City*, by Volkov, and the jacket informs me that it was only recently published in 1939. I'm thrilled that he has entrusted me with such a treasure, and I promise to take good care of it.

Hiding the book next to my heart in the folds of my coat, I hurry to catch up with my friends. I'm beside myself with happiness, but try to wear a look of indifference when I meet them outside, insisting that the teacher wanted nothing of importance.

I take my time reading the book, savoring every page, and picturing Ellie Smith and her dog, Totoshka, on their journey to the Emerald City, with the companions they meet on the way. I'm reluctant to share these precious moments, but overcoming my selfishness, I relate bits of the story to my brothers at bedtime, instead of my usual fairy tales. They are delighted by the witches and fantastical animals, and leave me in peace to read undisturbed, so that I will have another instalment for them at the end of the day.

Eventually, the time comes for me to return the book to Mikhail. I wait until class is dismissed, so that we can be alone.

'How did you enjoy the book, Tanya? What did you make of it?'

'It's difficult to explain in words the dissonance I'm experiencing. I have derived such pleasure from the book, but, at the same time, having the opportunity to read it has accentuated all that I'm missing – an entire world of books, plays, music, and art.'

'I understand completely. But tell me what impressed you about Ellie Smith and her friends?'

I take a little time to gather my thoughts.

'Throughout her time in Oz, Ellie is focused on getting home. Since she doesn't know how to do this herself, she seeks help from a variety of characters, including the good witches and the Wizard. Her goal is thwarted at every turn, but she never gives up. Whenever an obstacle is thrown in her path, she keeps calm and carries on. Failure is not an option. As for her companions, if they would only look inward, they would recognize their strengths, and understand that happiness and achievements are not dependent upon outside approval or gifts. It's what's on the inside that really counts.'

Mikhail is very quiet, and I fear I have made a fool of myself.

'I knew I made the right decision in choosing you, of all my students, to read the book,' he says at last.

Taking my hands in his he adds, 'I pray that you never forget these insights. In difficult times, think of Ellie Smith and her friends, and they will help you rise above despair. I'm certain that this dreadful exile will end, and that your courage, compassion and intelligence, like theirs, will eventually lead you home.'

I'm plucking up the courage to ask him why he's here in Siberia when he could be anywhere else. The question is on my lips when, suddenly, the room is lit up with flashing colors. Still holding my hand, Mikhail hurries us outside. My breath catches in my throat at the sight that awaits us. The most spectacular lights and swirls and rays fill the sky, dancing and darting here and there. I'm stunned by the grandeur of this dramatic, magical, otherworldly firework display.

'These are the Northern lights,' explains Mikhail, 'the Aurora Borealis. They are the result of collisions between gas particles in the earth's atmosphere with charged particles released from the sun's atmosphere. It's a phenomenon which only occurs near the magnetic North and South Poles.'

I watch in fascination as the entrancing, ever-changing lights curve and curl, flicker and slither. I'm moved to tears by the sheer beauty and wonder of this magical sight. Mikhail gently wipes them away.

'You see, Tanya, Siberia is not all bad. You would never have experienced this wonder of wonders if you had not been exiled here.'

I look up into his handsome face, illuminated by the lights, and I feel my heart will burst. He leans down and brushes my forehead with a fleeting kiss. The moment is more romantic than anything I have read in Erna's novels.

The celestial display comes to an end and, sadly, so does the magical interlude I have shared with Mikhail.

'You should go home, Tanya. Your family will be worried where you are.'

And, with a last squeeze of my hands, he sends me on my way. When I arrive at the hut, the boys jump on me with excitement.

'Tanya, did you see the fireworks? It was just like one of your fairy tales.'

Mama and Papa are also talking about the wondrous spectacle. I try to join in their excited chatter, but my mind is elsewhere. In my imagination I am picturing Mikhail as he comes to whisk me away to freedom. We ride off on one of the reindeer-drawn sleds, which are the only mode of transportation on the frozen river; or he comes for me in spring, when the river has thawed and the barges sail again. I am elated. I have something to look forward to. I have a dream.

All too soon, the dream becomes a nightmare. Several days later, officers from the NKVD, the People's Commisariat for Internal Affairs, barge into the classroom with a warrant for Mikhail's arrest. He is charged with fraternizing too closely with the prisoners, in particular with the Jews. Someone has informed on him. My classmates point the finger at Mr. Tatar, who openly despises him. I, however, have my own suspicions. One of the local girls saw me with Mikhail on the night of the Northern Lights. I have seen the look in her eyes, and recognized jealousy and animosity. I'm certain that she is the one responsible for Mikhail's terrible fate.

A petition is drawn up in Mikhail's defense, an appeal for his release, signed by everyone at school and most of the settlement. It is presented to the NKVD officers, but our pleas fall on deaf ears.

The following day, the entire community is gathered at the river's edge to witness Mikhail's departure. The air seems even colder than usual. My classmates are crying, and our tears freeze on our cheeks. As our breath rises in the air it turns to ice on our eyelashes and eyebrows. Several old men cough and spit, and their saliva drops to the ground as icy needles. The officers push Mikhail onto a reindeer-drawn sled, just like the one I imagined in my escape dreams, and they set off along the frozen river. My eyes lock with Mikhail's, and I see him mouth his final words to me: 'Remember Ellie Smith. Be strong.'

I watch as the sled becomes smaller and smaller in the distance, until I can no longer see it. This must be what it's like to attend the funeral of a loved one. It is, in fact, the funeral of my hopes and dreams. My heart is breaking.

Chapter 12

Spring and Summer, 1941

Following Mikhail's departure a depression enshrouds the settlement. My classmates are particularly miserable, having seen our beacon of hope disappearing over the horizon, taking with him our aspirations and prospects for the future. We are once again under the tutelage of the hated Mr. Tatar, and any remaining enthusiasm for study quickly dissipates. I have not shared my secret feelings for Mikhail, or the depth of my misery, with anyone. I long to confide in Erna, and I miss her even more acutely than before.

One morning, when I go down to the river to draw water, I bump into the Catholic priest who was instrumental in my recovery from anemia. Since my illness he has often approached me with a smile and a kind word, asking after my health.

'Why such a sad face, Tanya?' he asks me on this particular morning.

Reluctant to tell him of my broken heart, I simply reply that I can no longer bear the endless cold and gloom.

'Have a little more patience, my child. Spring is almost upon us. Soon you will hear an enormous boom, and you will know it has arrived.'

A couple of weeks later, we are awoken in the night by a colossal explosion. Mama and Papa huddle together in fright, drawing me and the boys in a tight embrace, thinking that the war has reached Siberia, and that the German bombers are once again threatening to kill us. The cabin shakes and the windows rattle.

'Maybe it's an earthquake and the ground is going to swallow us up,' cries Mama with a tremble in her voice.

'No, no,' I assure everyone joyously, remembering the priest's prediction.

'This is the sign that spring has arrived. It's the noise of the ice on the river starting to melt.'

The thaw does not happen overnight. Loud booms, crackling sounds and screeching noises, like an out-of-tune orchestra, continue to unsettle us for several weeks. As the thick layer of frozen water explodes it begins to move slowly, piling up mountainous columns of ice reaching several meters in height, and throwing them sideways. On each bank of the river, walls of ice tower majestically like fairy-tale glass castles, blocking our access to the water. As a result, we have to hack off pieces and melt them, until the towers thaw enough for the locals to cut a path to the river.

Winter is finally over. The temperatures rise, the river flows freely once again, and each day we check for the arrival of the first barges, in hopeful anticipation of more news from home, and perhaps another package. The promise of renewed contact with the outside world uplifts everyone's spirits, and even my own melancholia starts to abate.

When the first barge docks we do, indeed, receive a package, but it's not from home. It comes from our friends in Khodoriv. These good, kind people have not forgotten us. Mama opens the box, and we stare in wonderment and surprise at its contents: a box of *matzos* and some oil. The festival of Spring, Passover, must be imminent.

Since fleeing Poland we have had little or no means, or opportunity, to practice our Judaism. It hasn't been possible to obtain candles for Mama to light in welcoming the Sabbath; we haven't been able to observe the Sabbath properly since Papa has to work; Papa hasn't been able to calculate with any certainty exactly when the festivals fall, not even Yom Kippur, the most holy day of the year, when we are required to fast.

The box of matzos, indicating Passover's arrival, brings joy to our hearts mingled with painful nostalgia. The Seder meal on the first night of the festival was always particularly special for us children. The extended family, seated together around the dining table, would listen in wonder as Grandfather retold the story of the Israelites' exodus from Egypt, and, when prompted, the youngest among us would ask him *'Why is this night different from all other nights?'* We all grimaced as we ate the bitter herbs and salt water, representing the tears and the suffering of Pharaoh's Jewish slaves; after the meal we played a game of hide and seek, stealing a special piece of matzo, and bargaining with Grandfather for a reward in exchange for returning it to him.

Noting the sad expression on our faces, Papa assures us that we will have a marvelous Seder.

'I know the story by heart, and I am sure that you, Tanya'leh, remember how to ask and answer *'Why is this night different?'* We may not be able to eat a hearty meal, but there is no shortage here of bitter herbs,' he adds humorously.

Mama and Papa ask me to help them decide what to do with the matzos. Very few families have received their own supply, and there certainly aren't enough to last everyone for the eight days of the Passover festival. Together we decide to keep just enough for Mama, Papa, the boys and me to make the blessing and taste a piece at our Passover Seder. The remainder will be distributed to the elderly among us. Papa reasons that this might be their last Passover, and that it is our duty and privilege to give them the opportunity to perform this important ritual, which might give them both physical and spiritual nourishment.

Having counted two weeks since sighting the New Moon, Papa declares that Seder night has arrived. Mama has prepared what little she can under the circumstances.

'Children, let's pretend that we are sitting around our large dining table at home. The tablecloth is pure white, and Tanya and I have laid out the beautiful porcelain dishes, silver cutlery and the crystal wine goblets. Look,' she says, pointing to an imaginary spot, 'there is the Seder plate displaying six items which remind us of the Passover story. Who can tell us what they are?'

Dovid is too young to remember the last Passover we celebrated, but Jozef can recall most of the objects. Conjuring up past memories he says, 'There is a shank bone and a burnt hard-boiled egg.'

'Well done,' says Papa. 'They represent burnt offerings which used to be brought to the Temple in Jerusalem. What else?'

'There's some sweet stuff and some bitter stuff,' replies Jozef.

Papa explains, '*Charoseth*, made of apples, nuts and wine, reminds us of the bricks and mortar the Israelite slaves were forced to make; and the very bitter horseradish, which brings tears to our eyes, represents the hardships they endured. The fifth item, lettuce, is a second reminder of those bitter times.'

Seeing that Jozef's contribution has finished, I add, 'The last item is parsley, which we dip in salt water to remind us of the slaves' tears.'

'We have some bitter herbs,' says Mama. 'And instead of parsley I have managed to get potato.'

Papa begins to recount from memory the Passover story of the Ten Plagues, the parting of the Red Sea, and Moses leading the Israelites out of Egypt. After a few minutes, he turns to me.

'Tanya'leh, now it's time for you to ask the four questions.'

'No, Papa,' I reply. 'I'm not the youngest. We have a surprise for you.'

I have been teaching little Dovid the four questions in secret. When he stands and recites the first one, Mama's and Papa's faces light up with delight. He does a great job, with a little prompting by me, of asking all four questions, while we all join in answering them.

We eat our matzo, the unleavened bread of affliction, and Jozef performs an elaborate pantomime of eating the traditional chicken soup and matzo balls, making us all laugh, even though it is sorely missed at our Siberian Seder table. When Papa finishes telling the story, we recite together the blessing which is the culmination of every Seder.

'Today we are slaves, but next year we will be free in Jerusalem.'

This year those words are more meaningful than ever before.

As usual, Papa was right in his decision to give most of our matzos to the elderly. My friend Sarah's grandfather was weak from hunger, and the small amount of matzo he received was not enough to give him physical strength, but we are told that his eyes brimmed with tears of joy as he recited the blessing before eating it. On the last day of Passover he died.

Now that we have contact with the outside world, snippets of news start to reach the community. In July, we learn that the Germans have attacked the Soviet Union in a huge military operation, which inflicted heavy losses on Russian forces. The Germans were advancing fast, and the Russians were conscripting men of every age to reinforce their troops at the Front. One day, army officials arrive and inform the settlement that, if their parents agree, young men born in Russia will be granted full pardons and conscripted. In return, their families will be allowed to leave as well.

Papa has another one of his prophetic dreams.

'I saw Grandfather beckoning to me from the deck of a ship,' he tells Mama.

'Do you see any ships here, apart from those taking away the soldiers?' Mama asks sarcastically.

'If he showed me a ship,' counters Papa, 'it's a sign that I must take my family away from here. We are weak and with no reserves. We will not survive another winter in this place.'

Without wasting any time, Papa springs into action. He gathers up anything and everything which can be sold or exchanged. He forbids us to tell our friends or neighbors of our preparations, so as not to raise suspicion, or alert them to our plans. When the last barge arrives to transport the remaining soldiers, Papa uses the money he has accumulated to bribe the captain to assist in our escape, and we are secreted aboard in the dead of night. The captain instructs us to remain hidden until the barge is far enough away from the settlement to be out of sight.

At dawn, the barge pulls away from the dock, and, miraculously, we escape. Mama, trembling with anxiety, holds the boys close and keeps them quiet. As soon as there is sufficient distance between us and the settlement, we emerge cautiously from our hiding place and drink in the air of freedom. We are homeless and penniless, but, once again, Papa lifts his eyes towards heaven and mouths 'thank you' to Grandfather for showing him the way forward.

The first port of call is Bodaybo, where we disembark from the barge.

'We will go in search of the town's Jewish residents,' says Papa 'and see what news they have.'

Having found out where the Jews live, we make our way

there. Papa approaches a couple of men, who update him on the state of the war and the German invasion of Russia. Since the radio broadcasts are censored, everyone is skeptical as to the authenticity of the reports, but it's clear to all that the pact between Stalin and Hitler has evaporated into thin air. Papa is very concerned about what this will mean for Poland. Sadly, they have no news from home for us.

Mama looks surprised when I ask if, by any chance, anyone knows the fate of the teacher Mikhail, and I blush under her scrutiny. To my astonishment they reply that they do. Unexpectedly, he wasn't sent to stand trial, and has been spared conviction. My relief is short-lived, however, when they explain that instead he has been conscripted and posted to the Russian Front.

'You will be able to write to your classmates and let them know that he is safe,' says Mama stupidly.

'Safe? What can possibly be safe about the Russian Front?'

If I had harbored any hopes of seeing him again, I now know for sure that he is lost to me forever.

Several families offer us accommodation and encourage us to stay, but Papa is determined to put as much distance as possible between us and the approaching Siberian winter, so we continue our journey on the barge. Mama is miserable as she is still plagued with sea sickness. A number of days pass, and several of the children on board fall ill. Fever and sore throat are accompanied by diarrhea and vomiting. When a couple of days later a rash appears, I see the troubled faces of the parents as the whisper passes from one to another, '*scarlet fever*'. The young are weak from hunger and from the journey, and many quickly succumb. One by one the number of the dead and dying grows, and almost every morning a small body is lowered over the side of the barge to its watery grave.

I can see that Mama and Papa are sick with fear and, praying for our good health, try to keep us as far away as possible from the infected. For several days they believe that their prayers have been answered, until Jozef and Dovid awaken one morning covered in the tell-tale red rash.

Chapter 13

Life in Ust-Kut, 1942

When the journey by river comes to an end, we disembark in Ust-Kut. From the barge's final destination it would be necessary to travel by truck, as we had done on our way to Siberia, to the next river and our onward journey. Papa decides that this overland trip would be too arduous for the boys, and that our first priority is to find a hospital where they can be treated.

Winter is around the corner, already announcing its imminent arrival with gusty winds and rain. We are all shivering with cold, the boys quaking uncontrollably because of the high fevers they are running. Mama goes from house to house imploring the owners to allow us a corner in which to get warm. As soon as they see the sick boys, they close their doors in her face, shutting out the risk of infection. On the brink of desperation, we finally come to a small farmhouse occupied by a lone farmer, who takes pity on us and lets us in. He explains to Papa that there's a hospital a short distance away, and he kindly offers to take us there as soon as we have rested.

The hospital consists of one doctor and a few beds. The doctor examines the boys, and solemnly announces that they are suffering from pneumonia, a complication of the scarlet fever. When they are tucked up in bed, with Mama lying at their feet, Papa whispers in my ear '*Shelter, Sustenance, Survival,*' and asks the farmer to take us into town to look for somewhere to live and for employment.

In what passes for a poor man's town hall, an official asks Papa what his trade is.

'Foodstuffs,' Papa replies, causing the official to smile broadly and clap his hands.

'This must be providence. You are exactly what we need here. Just across the river is a food factory, which produces supplies for the soldiers at the Front. Production is at an all-time high, but we have no one with knowledge and experience to run the place. If you'd like the job of Manager, it's yours.'

Well, of course, Papa accepts, and the very next day, he takes over the factory.

For a couple of weeks, the boys are very sick. Mama is distraught with anxiety.

'If only Doctor Berish were here,' she wails over and over like a madwoman. 'We need Doctor Berish.'

Berish was Mama's late grandfather, a *mekubbal* – a scholar and practitioner of the Kabbalah, an ancient wisdom steeped in Jewish mysticism. He had possessed the gift of healing, and was called to help patients for whom doctors could find no remedy. He had also practiced hypnotism, and exaggerated stories of his wizardry circulated around town. His success as a natural healer was well known, and almost every Jewish family in Tsanz, and many gentiles too, had, for one reason or another, procured his services, for which this righteous man refused to take money. Of course, by now he had been dead for many years, and I have no recollection of him, but Mama told me that when I was very young I contracted severe pneumonia and was not expected to live. Doctor Berish bled me with leeches, administered other natural remedies, placed his hands over me, and chanted prayers. Thanks to his ministrations, I survived.

A third bed in the boys' room is occupied by a farmer's son. His mother can only visit from time to time because she has to work. Mama strikes a deal with her.

'If you bring me a chicken, I will prepare a nourishing soup, and in return I'll look after your son, and tend to him when you are unable to come.'

Mama feeds the hearty soup to the three boys. She washes them, administers compresses, and reads to them. Little by little they begin to improve, but it takes a long while before they regain their strength and make a full recovery.

While Mama is at the hospital attending the sick, it falls to me to look after Papa. I cook, clean and do laundry, and every day I stand in line for bread and other provisions. While I'm learning a lot of life lessons, I can't attend school this year. By the time we are settled in Ust-Kut and the boys have recovered, the school year is half way through and I'm refused admission.

Every morning, Papa takes a boat across the river to the factory. In addition to a meager wage, he is allocated a small allowance of foodstuffs, flour, sugar and the like, which he is permitted to bring home for the family, and for the first time in a very long while we are no longer starving. Papa has also forged new friendships with some of the locals, who are very kind to us. From time to time, someone arrives at our door with a fish from his catch, or part of an animal hunted in the forest. They give us invaluable advice on how to survive the climate and how to conform to the local customs.

We are living in a house which is divided into two identical halves by a thin wooden partition, providing one room for our family and one for our neighbors. In contrast to the dirt floor in our cabin in the settlement, this house has the luxury of wooden flooring. But the most marvelous surprise in our new home is electricity. Every house has one electric light, and this wonder of wonders compensates for all the other deprivations.

Against one wall stands a large stone stove for cooking and heating, while much of the rest of the room is taken up by three pallets. I sleep on one, Mama and Papa on the second, and the boys on the third. We possess very few clothes, and the little we have hangs unceremoniously on nails sticking out from one wall. One corner of the room is home to two buckets of water for cooking and washing. These need refilling every day, and once again it becomes my job to be water-carrier. The buckets are suspended at each end of a long pole, which is slung across my shoulders. Once the buckets are full, I slowly trudge back to the house under the yoke of my heavy burden. For the first few difficult days, I suffer painfully from the load I'm shouldering, and slop water as I shift my weight from foot to foot. Luckily, our house, like most of the others here, is located in close proximity to the river, and now that I have become accustomed to the task, I manage the short distance quite easily.

The family occupying the other half of the house comprises a middle aged, stocky blond woman, Yulya, her son, Pyotr, who is a year younger than me, her twenty-something daughter, Anya, and son-in-law, Oleg. We call Anya's husband 'the Pilot', because, when Papa asked him his trade, he boasted that in Moscow he had been a test pilot of fighter aircraft. He related in heart-stopping detail, how on one of his flights a malfunction caused the plane to spin out of control and crash. By some miracle he walked away from the debris unscathed. Fearing an investigation and tribunal, he fled to Siberia, into anonymity, reinforced by a change of name and family. In all probability he has deserted a wife and children in Moscow. In Russian there is an adage 'wherever I live I have a wife'. Embracing this saying, he married Anya. Anya is an attractive girl with a slightly oriental look about her, enhanced by almond-shaped eyes and long, shiny black hair which she weaves into a thick, heavy braid.

Our neighbors' peculiar lifestyle both fascinates and frightens us. Yulya tells us that her husband, Boris, had managed a factory somewhere in the Balkans. Apparently, for reasons he could not explain, and she could not comprehend, he had made an enemy of one of the workers, who informed on him to the authorities, accusing him of some fabricated crime. Consequently, the family was exiled to Siberia, and Boris was shipped off to a faraway slave labor camp. Every evening, Yulya performs a creepy ritual, sitting by the fire and crumpling up pieces of paper, which she throws into the flames. When the paper begins to curl, writhe, and glow as it turns to black ash, Yulya stares at it in trance-like concentration.

'Look, I can see my husband,' she proclaims excitedly, pointing at the dancing embers.

'There he is, pushing a wheelbarrow. He is alive!'

Each time she visualizes the poor man performing one back-breaking task or another. It's quite ghoulish and gruesome to witness this intelligent, educated woman practicing her mumbo-jumbo. Somehow, it seems to bring her comfort. Her husband's fate has made her wary and suspicious of others, so that while she's polite and helpful to our family, she continues to treat us like strangers, tempering her behavior with caution. Under Stalin's terror regime, everyone speaks in hushed whispers, suspicious that a harmless-seeming neighbor might be the next whistleblower.

Oleg, Anya's husband, habitually gets drunk. When he returns home intoxicated and violent, he invariably seeks out their pet dog, and begins to kick it mercilessly. And then the pandemonium starts. As he beats the poor animal, he curses in Russian at the top of his voice; the dog barks and whimpers, while Yulya and Anya scream at him to stop. Anya wails and begs him, 'Please tell me you have not been cursing your superiors or your manager. What will befall us if they cart you off to prison?' Worse still, she is frequently the one to bear the brunt of his punches and kicks. Once Oleg has discharged all his anger and frustration, he calms down, and the women put him to bed where he lays singing songs well into the night.

On our side of the partition, the boys and I can hear the goings on, and, much to Mama's dismay, our Russian vocabulary has been augmented to include several choice swear words. While we wait for the ruckus to stop, we lay quietly in our beds, frightened of making any noise which might attract Oleg's attention.

There are other nights, however, when the silence on their side of the partition is broken by grunting noises, and the rhythmic creaking of the bed nearest to us, which is shared by Oleg and Anya. Thanks to Erna's '*lessons*' I'm well aware of what the sounds mean, and try my best to shut them out. I can't, however, suppress my dreams, in which I fantasize about Mikhail's passionate lovemaking, his lips on mine, his hands caressing my body, while I surrender to his manhood.

My family's situation in Ust-Kut is quite unusual. While the other women in our neighborhood leave early each morning for work, Mama stays home to look after Jozef and Dovid, claiming fragile physical and emotional health. She rarely leaves the house. In addition to her usual snobbishness, she despises the Russians, she hates the town, and she is utterly miserable. She also abhors standing in queues. However, soon after we were settled, Mama learned that when some sought-after item or other is rumored to have arrived in town, a member of every family rushes in the direction of the distribution point.

On one occasion, a consignment of felt shoes arrived, and Mama did not want to miss out on them. As soon as the rumor of their availability spread, a huge snake-like queue formed. Mama had to wait in line for almost three hours. She returned in a state of shock, not from the length of the queue, however, but rather from the conversation started by some of the women.

'That is the last time I stand in line,' she exclaimed angrily.

'You will not believe what those prying women asked me.'

When she had my attention, she continued.

'One woman had the nerve to enquire how many children I have. I replied that I have three. And then they asked me how many of my children had died.'

Mama said that when she answered that none had died, the women congratulated her on her good fortune. Seeing her puzzled expression, they explained that in Ust-Kut almost half the newborn babies die.

'As soon as the baby is born, its mother is required to return to work. The infant is placed in a crèche where conditions are inadequate and disease is easily passed from one to another. The mortality rate is very high.'

Mama said that one of the women took an accusatory tone, suggesting that her children had not died since she did not go to work. Mama was adamant.

'I refuse to be subjected to any further interrogations, or to be told any more horror stories,' she declared.

From that day on, queueing became my responsibility. I love it. Sometimes, I have to stand for two or three hours, but I relish the time, listening to all the gossip and rumors, stories, and conversations around me. By eavesdropping, I am learning a lot from these women about life and love, natural medicine, handicrafts, and, most of all, how to remain optimistic, even under the most trying of circumstances.

In order to fill my days, since I can't go to school, I frequent the town library. My Russian is now quite fluent, and I quickly work my way through the small collection of books the library has to offer, until there comes a point when there's very little left for me to read. So I'm downhearted when the day comes for me to return the last available book. But when I arrive, a wonderful surprise awaits me.

The building next to the library has been commandeered to serve as an annex, to house books, magazines and other items evacuated from the State Library in Leningrad. The librarian explains that since Leningrad is besieged by the Germans, the invaluable contents of the library are under constant threat of bombing. While it was still possible, some of the collections have been spirited away to libraries far from the endangered city.

Overseeing this treasure is a tall, blond woman, who looks like she's on the brink of starvation. I approach her and introduce myself.

'Hello. My name is Tanya. I spend a lot of time at the library and have read everything in its catalog. Would it be possible for me to borrow some reading material from this collection?'

'I am very pleased to meet you Tanya. My name is Svetlana, and I will be happy to lend you some books,' she replies in her soft-spoken, cultured voice.

'But it must be our secret.'

Under Svetlana's attentive tutelage, I'm introduced to Tolstoy, Dostoyevsky, Chekhov, and the cream of the Russian classics.

Wishing to express her appreciation to Svetlana for taking me under her wing, and show her hospitality, Mama invites her for dinner one evening. I describe to Mama Svetlana's emaciated appearance, so she goes to great pains to obtain some wholesome ingredients and prepare a nourishing meal. When we sit down to dinner and Mama places a plate of chicken and vegetables in front of Svetlana, our guest's eyes well up with tears of disbelief and gratitude. While Svetlana eats slowly, savoring every mouthful, she describes in horrifying detail the state of affairs in Leningrad.

'The German forces have completely surrounded the city, severing all lines of communication and transportation.

Supplies cannot get through and the city's food stocks have been badly depleted. I have heard that people are hunting dogs and cats for food, and there are even stories of cannibalism. Oil and coal supplies are exhausted, meaning that the city is without any central heating, and people are burning furniture and floorboards, in order to keep warm in the intensely frigid weather. Citizens are dying in droves of starvation and of cold, and corpses litter the streets. The city is under constant bombardment. The noise is deafening and the destruction brutal.'

Papa and Mama listen to Svetlana's monologue, with growing concern evident on their faces.

'If this is the fate of a great city such as Leningrad,' says Papa, 'I shudder to think what has befallen Nowy Sącz.'

I sincerely empathize with Svetlana, but, at the same time, I find it ironic that the free citizens of Leningrad are in an even worse situation than we had been in the Siberian prison camp.

Spring finally arrives, and we rejoice at having survived another Siberian winter. Mama cultivates vegetables in a small garden area behind the house, and Papa manages to obtain a few chickens, providing us with the luxury of fresh eggs. We consider ourselves very fortunate indeed.

When school summer vacation begins, our neighbor Yulya approaches me.

'It's a shame that you missed the school year, Tanya. Do you know that during the summer special courses are taught in the school for those who failed exams at the end of the year? Why don't you attend? If you study hard and pass the exams you will be able to enter school in autumn at the next grade level. You are a bright girl with enough knowledge to sail through easily.'

Papa, of course, encourages me to do as Yulya suggests. With her help, in less than two months I cover all the material and take the exams, achieving excellent grades. My place in school for the coming year is guaranteed. Life is looking up.

Chapter 14

Moving on, 1942

I was excitedly preparing for the first day of school when I noticed that Papa wore that look on his face once again.

'It's time for us to move on,' he announced one evening.

'But, Papa,' I protested, 'we are settled here, and I'm about to start school. You were the one who encouraged me to study over the summer. What was the point if I am to miss yet another year? Please don't uproot us again.'

But Papa's mind was made up.

'We must try to make our way to a more central region, with communication to the outside world and railway connections.'

This was easier said than done, however. Without special papers it was forbidden to travel from one place to another, and Papa spent a great deal of his time and energy trying to procure them. Finally, a truck driver who brought supplies to Papa's factory agreed, for a fee, to produce the necessary documents for all of us, recommending that we travel to Nizhneudinsk on the Uda River.

'The town is a stop on the Trans-Siberian Railway line, and I know of a food factory there run by a Jew who will surely help you,' he tells us.

And so, at the beginning of autumn, we're on the move once again. Papa dispatches letters to home and to Khodoriv, asking for news, and apprising relatives and friends of our plans. We pack up our few belongings, bid our neighbors farewell, and set off for the umpteenth time towards the unknown.

Initially, as we climb aboard the driver's truck, the boys are excited by this new adventure, but in common with most children of their age, they quickly lose their patience, and begin to nag, asking when we will arrive at our destination. As usual, it's left to me to try to keep them occupied and distracted.

The driver estimates that the first leg of our journey is about two hundred and fifty kilometers. But as we must travel on secondary roads rather than highways, the going is excruciatingly slow. The road is uneven, with many twists and turns. Mama, who has already demonstrated her propensity for travel sickness, suffers from the turbulence in the truck, as it bounces along the tortuous route, which is punctuated by potholes. Around us, the truck's tarpaulin cover flaps noisily in the wind, letting in the cold and drowning out the conversation, such as it is.

After three days of discomfiture, we arrive at our first destination point, on the Angara River. Anxiously, Papa turns to the driver.

'I'm worried we won't be able to make the river journey before the water freezes, and then what will we do?'

The driver puts his mind at rest.

'Have no fear; this section of the Angara is the only Siberian waterway that flows freely even in winter.'

Bidding him farewell, we set out for our next port of call. I'm delighted to leave the claustrophobic confines of the truck and set sail, but Mama, barely recovered from the road journey, is overcome, once again, by motion sickness brought on by the listing of the barge in the river's strong current.

The skies are blue and the air crisp. The outside temperature has not yet fallen below zero, but any warmth from the weak sunshine is diluted by the wind created by the boat's progress. One bank of the wide river rolls gently towards the water's edge; on the other side undulating, sparsely wooded hills plunge sharply into the depths, disappearing below their reflection in the sparkling water.

Here and there, I spot a lone fisherman, or sometimes a group, endeavoring to catch an evening meal. I point them out to Jozef, recalling our angling lessons during our summer vacation in Szczawnica. How I long for the taste of fresh fish. There and then I determine that somehow, in our next home, fish will regularly feature on the menu.

Following two days on the river, and a further two hundred kilometers in yet another truck, we arrive stiff and exhausted in Nizhneudinsk. The city is not particularly large, but we discover that it is an important stop on the route of the Trans-Siberian Railway, because of its proximity to the nearby Biryusa gold mines.

We begin an exploration of the town. Starting out along the main thoroughfare, we haven't gone very far when we reach one of the town's largest and tallest buildings.

'Look, Papa,' I call out in amazement, pointing to the façade above the entrance.

An elegant inscription testifies to the building's inauguration as the town's synagogue, in May 1914.

'Such a prominent synagogue must indicate a sizeable Jewish community in the town,' Papa says confidently.

We enter the impressive brick edifice, marveling at the ornate interior; the walls are embellished with arched alcoves, and the middle of its high ceiling is embossed with an elaborate star-shaped gilded medallion. However, as we look around, we notice that there is no evidence of religious artifacts; no candelabra, no prayer books, no Torah scrolls, not even a rabbi's pulpit. Papa finds a janitor in one of the side rooms, and is disappointed to learn from the fellow that, like all the other synagogues in the Soviet Union, this one has been closed for some twenty years. It has been converted into an administration building.

Following more detective work, Papa succeeds in obtaining the details of the Jewish factory owner, Isak Gurevich. As our truck driver predicted, Mr. Gurevich welcomes us, and offers to help us settle in. He finds us a small vacant house, and introduces us to several other Jewish refugee families, who have drifted here from central Russia, from the Ukraine, and from the farther reaches of Siberia.

What a luxury to have a house entirely to ourselves; no partition, and no peculiar neighbors. Of course, there is still no running water, and we have to use an outhouse in the garden, and draw water from a well. But we have electricity, and we each have our own bed. Mr. Gurevich appoints Papa factory manager, and finally there's enough money for extra clothing and food, including fish.

Papa is satisfied – the three esses: *Shelter, sustenance, survival*, have been taken care of.

In addition to this massive improvement in our situation, I can finally attend school. Thanks to the certificate conferred upon me at the end of the summer in Ust-Kut, I'm accepted into the next grade. I'm determined to concentrate and study hard, making up for all the disruptions and lost time since leaving Tsanz.

'I will make Mikhail proud of me,' I tell myself.

While I'm reasonably certain that academically I'll fit in well at the school, socially it's a much greater challenge. It turns out that I'm the only Jewish girl in my class, and my classmates are suspicious of me. My manners and dress are different to theirs; I don't curse (despite knowing how to, thanks to Oleg); and I avoid physical familiarity with the others girls, who are always hugging and touching each other during and after class. Ever since the appallingly cramped conditions in the cattle trucks on our journey to Siberia, I jealously guard my personal space, and shy away from unnecessary physical contact. They consider me a misfit, an odd bird, and call me '*Princessa*'. They're not unpleasant or cruel, but make it quite clear that I'm an outsider.

I do manage to forge a friendship of sorts with the chemistry teacher's son, Alexei, on a *quid pro quo* basis. Math is certainly not my strongest subject, and Alexei has difficulty with language, so we develop a mutually beneficial tutoring arrangement. Things are going well until one afternoon as we walk home from school, I reprimand him for wiping his nose on some plants growing at the side of the road.

'That's disgusting,' I tell him. 'Where are your manners and breeding?'

Offended, he replies, 'You people think you are so cultured. What's so cultured about wiping your nose on a piece of cloth, screwing it up in a ball, and putting it in your pocket, to be carried around for the rest of the day?'

I grudgingly admit to myself that he has a point, and resolve to try to be more tolerant of my classmates' ways, and to try to gain their acceptance.

Because of the war, a number of compulsory activities have been introduced into the school curriculum. Extra emphasis is put on sports and physical fitness. We are taught First Aid, and how to take apart and reassemble certain weapons. I remember

Papa's advice on our first day in the Siberian camp, to embrace new knowledge and skills, however irrelevant they may seem at the time, and I pay close attention.

We are also required to volunteer at the town's hospital. Being on the main railway line, Nizhneudinsk has become a treatment center for wounded *frontoviks*, soldiers posted at the Front. The Russian forces are taking a beating, and the hospital staff is unable to cope with the heavy number of casualties.

We're happy to help out and do whatever we can to contribute to the war effort. In addition to rolling bandages, cleaning floors, running errands, and the like, we put on silly plays to entertain those recovering from their wounds; we sing songs and dance; we read books aloud; and we help to feed those who are unable to feed themselves.

On one particular evening there is a power outage, and I'm needed to provide illumination for the surgeons, by holding up a kerosene lamp next to the operating table. This is the first time I'm witnessing surgery, and I have to fight hard not to faint or vomit, or let my arm shake when it becomes tired from holding the lamp.

The operation stretches on and on, and I don't hold out much hope for the patient. There is blood everywhere, its metallic scent pervading the air, exposed intestines, and embedded pieces of shrapnel threatening vital organs. At the end of the ordeal, I'm amazed that the doctors consider the surgery successful, and the medical team praises and thanks me for my fortitude and contribution to the effort.

'Perhaps, Tanya,' one of the surgeons suggests, 'you might consider nursing as a career.'

I'd be lying if I were to deny being exceptionally proud of myself, and I take great delight in recounting the details when I arrive home. But the experience has taught me that I definitely have no desire to study medicine.

Many of the town's menfolk have been conscripted into the army, leaving a depleted work force in the coal mines, lumber mills, and cotton fields. Here too, my schoolmates and I are called upon to pull our weight, and a roster is drawn up. I shudder as I recall the harsh labor in the Siberian prison camp, and am relieved when I'm sent to work in the cotton fields, rather than in the woods or the mines. My relief is short-lived, however. I suffer a serious allergic reaction to the cotton seeds and fluff, which flutter in the air, penetrating ears, noses and eyes. At first, this causes mild discomfort, but after several days my eyes become inflamed and swollen shut. I'm in dreadful pain, I can't sleep, and I'm petrified that I'm going blind.

'Mama, do something,' I cry out, pushing away her hand, as she pours water over my eyes, in the hope of soothing them.

A neighbor, who has heard of my plight, offers Mama an herbal poultice.

'This will soothe her pain,' she says, 'and speed up her recovery.'

Thankfully, the poultice does help; my eyes slowly recover and I regain my sight. I am never required to pick cotton again.

As the first few months pass and I make an effort to fit in, I gain the respect of my classmates, and when elections are held for class president, much to my amazement I'm chosen. I imagine that this so-called honor will afford me privileges, but, to my dismay, I discover that the appointment merely amounts to being in charge of decorum, cleanliness, and order within the classroom. For a majority of the time this doesn't present a problem, but it's not all smooth sailing.

There's one particularly overactive and disobedient boy in the class, Arkady. He's not a good student, and finds it hard to conform to the strict Russian school regimen. I have developed a good rapport with him, and can usually calm him down, but there are times when his behavior is beyond my control. On one particular occasion, Arkady is called to task by the teacher for not completing an assignment as instructed. His reaction is to tear his paper to shreds and throw the pieces at her, before storming out of the room. We all wait in stunned silence to hear what terrible punishment would befall him.

'Tanya,' the teacher calls in her steely voice.

'You are responsible for this class, and you have failed in your duty. You will stay after school and wash the entire top floor of the building.'

In astonishment, I protest, 'but that will take until midnight, Miss Zhukova.'

She merely shrugs.

'Then perhaps you will learn to take your responsibilities more seriously in the future.'

I'm not afraid of the strenuous task. I do most of the chores at home, cleaning the house and the latrine, and fetching water. Now that Jozef has grown a little he shares some of the work with me, but I'm by no means living the spoiled, comfortable life of a *Princessa*. No, it's not the cleaning that bothers me, but the stinging feeling of humiliation and unfairness. Why should I be responsible for the fact that Miss Zhukova is unable to control one misbehaving boy in her classroom? Isn't it her job to engage and interest each student, however challenging?

When school's finished for the day, I trudge my way upstairs to begin my punishment. After a few minutes, I hear noise on the stairs. To my astonishment, one by one my classmates, including Arkady, appear, and insist on sharing the work.

'We elected you so we must take the blame for your inadequacies,' they rationalize, waving aside my objections.

Arkady even apologizes for getting me into trouble. This unexpected show of camaraderie makes me feel that finally I'm no longer the outsider.

There are those who continue to treat me coolly, and one girl in particular has been trying to make trouble for me whenever possible. Her name is Galina. She has a crush on Alexei, and is very jealous of my friendship with him. I, of course, have no interest in him romantically; no one can supplant Mikhail in my heart. But she believes what she thinks she sees between us, and is green with envy.

One morning when I open my desk, I discover that the leads of all my pencils have been broken off. On another occasion, Galina 'accidentally' pours water into my gym shoes while we're changing for our sports lesson. And then there's the day when she brushes past me, holding the blackboard eraser with which she peppers my cardigan in white chalk.

Unimpressed by her lack of ingenuity – I could have thought up far more novel, interesting and effective stunts – I display an indifference, which quickly wipes the smirk of satisfaction off her face. Every time she pulls something, I get my revenge by fawning over Alexei, whispering in his ear and sharing a private joke, all of which have the desired effect of infuriating her. Eventually, I grow tired of this game.

'Alexei,' I say one afternoon. 'You do realize that Galina has a crush on you, don't you?'

Alexei blushes. 'I suppose I do, but I have no idea what to do about it.'

Puzzled, I ask him whether he would like me to shoo her away, and I'm surprised when he replies, 'Absolutely not. I want you to help me make her my girl.'

This is my first attempt at matchmaking – and not a very

challenging one, I must admit. I strike a bargain with Galina.

'If you stop your nastiness,' I tell her, 'I will put in a good word for you with Alexei. I can't promise he will be interested, but I'll see what I can do.'

After that it's child's play to get them together. While Galina and I are still not friends, there is, at least, a truce between us.

No one comes near to filling Erna's role of best friend, but I do have one close friendship with a girl called Ola. She's the daughter of the postmaster, whom Papa badgers on a daily basis, hoping for replies to the letters we have been sending home. Papa is becoming increasingly worried about this absence of communication. I wish some word would arrive to put our minds at rest.

Ola is a very pleasant, sweet-natured girl, with large brown, laughing eyes, set in a chubby-cheeked face. We often prepare for exams together, and sometimes I stay overnight at her house. Her family keeps a cow in their back yard, and there's no shortage of butter and cream at their table, which accounts for the family's plump proportions.

In the middle of the first night that I spend at Ola's, I'm awakened by a commotion coming from the kitchen. I make my way cautiously downstairs, and find the entire family seated around the dining table. Ola's mother is serving up a hearty Russian soup, thick with all manner of vegetables and grains, to which she has added cream. Each individual has his or her own spoon, but the soup is eaten collectively from one huge communal bowl.

'What's the occasion?' I ask Ola, bleary-eyed, half believing that I'm sleepwalking in a particularly vivid dream.

'This is not a special occasion, Tanya.'

'It's our custom that if someone wakes up hungry in the

middle of the night, the entire household gets up, and everyone gathers around the table to eat a meal.'

This is the strangest custom I have ever witnessed. No wonder they are all teetering on the edge of obesity!

Now that I'm accepted by my school mates, I'm determined to hasten my integration into community life. With this in mind, I decide to apply to join the *Komsomol*, the All-Union Leninist Young Communist League. I'm so proud when I receive my red party membership card. I join in enthusiastically with various youth activities, attending meetings, and even learning some of the songs.

Thank you Comrade Stalin
For our happy life!
For our happy childhood
For our wonderful days

I become quite sympathetic towards some of the social and political ideas espoused by the party, and even, believe it or not, learn to admire Stalin. Of course, I balk at the party's fierce anti-religion ideology.

In one of my many discussions with Svetlana, the librarian in Ust-Kut, I asked why the communists were so against religious practice.

'The library has a whole section of books on the topic, Tanya,' she replied, and recommended that I read some of them, in order to understand the Soviet Union's official doctrine of atheism, and Lenin's assertion that *'Religion is the opium of the people'*.

I devoured critiques on the various theologies, from Christianity to Islam and Hindu, and of course Judaism, learning firstly about the principles underpinning them, and then examining the Russian arguments 'proving' their erroneousness and illogicality. My reading reinforced my conviction that religion is an important concept, and that belief in an intangible, ethical, divine being is more logical than the superstitions and amulets I have witnessed the Russians clinging to. I vowed that if sometime in the future circumstances permitted, I would return to my birthright and raise my children in a practicing, Jewish home.

Winter in Nizhneudinsk is as harsh as in the rest of Siberia, but here, at least, we have warm clothes, sufficient food, and electricity. However, our 'war studies' at school include long marches in the snow; my cheeks freeze, and I can't feel my fingers and toes. Our teacher, who was wounded at the Front and dispatched to our town to prepare students for future eventualities, tends to be lenient with me, and lends a hand when he sees that the challenges are too difficult for me.

He explained to the others, 'Tanya is not hardy like you. She is not used to this climate and we must help her.'

Ola laughingly replied, 'Don't spoil her. She must learn to cope. Otherwise she will turn into a capitalist.'

As spring turns to summer, Papa begins to consider moving on again. The Polish People's Army has been formed to fight alongside Soviet troops, and the government has loosened restrictions of movement for Polish citizens in Russia. We are now rid of our convict status, and free to determine where to live. Naturally, we still require travel papers, and Papa has approached Mr. Gurevich to request permission to leave, and to obtain the necessary documentation. He doesn't wish to appear ungrateful for our friend's support and generosity when we arrived in Nizhneudinsk, so he explains with a measure of exaggeration that Mama is unwell, and that he fears her condition will deteriorate if she has to endure another Siberian winter.

'My plan is to take my family to central Asia in search of a warmer climate,' he tells Mr. Gurevich.

Secretly, he confides in me.

'Tanya, it's my hope that if we settle close to the Persian border, it might be possible to sneak across out of Russia, and somehow make our way to Palestine.'

This time I don't object to leaving, although I will miss Ola, Alexei, and even Miss Zhukova. But, if we can indeed reach Eretz Israel...

Chapter 15

Tajikistan, 1943-1945

For the umpteenth time, we packed up our belongings, and bid farewell to yet another group of friends we'll never see again. We were all excited to leave Siberia behind us, but Papa neglected to mention that the distance to our new destination was more than four thousand kilometers. The journey was interminable, tedious and uncomfortable.

We traveled in abominable conditions for what seemed like weeks, waiting for hours, and often days, for a train connection from one remote stop to another. There didn't appear to be any regular schedules or timetables, and the trains were old, crowded and smelly, but nonetheless luxurious compared to the cattle trucks that transported us from Ukraine to Siberia. And there were no armed guards keeping us under lock and key.

As we progressed southwards, the passengers' body heat, combined with the rising temperatures outside, turned the crowded space into a stuffy oven. At least this time we had a plentiful supply of water, and the opportunity to climb down and stretch our legs whenever the train pulled into a station. There were no sleeping compartments, and the best we could do was to doze off sitting up, awakened every time a curve in the tracks toppled us sideways into our neighbor.

We were not the only ones fleeing Siberia. Thousands of refugees put the cold behind them, and surged southwards in search of warmth. Unlike my family, however, most had not had the opportunity to recover their strength, and they made the journey weakened by the ravages of starvation and the inhuman conditions of the previous years. On arrival in the hot Asian climate, they quickly succumbed to typhus and diphtheria, and unknown tropical diseases, falling like flies, and dying in large numbers.

Thankfully, during our stay in Nizhneudinsk we ate well and put some flesh on our skeletal bodies. We replenished our vitamins, built up our reserves, and our immune systems were strong enough to ward off infection.

The passing countryside was a monotonous waste of steppe grassland and desert, stretching as far as the eye could see, towards an endless horizon, punctuated here and there by a group of wild horses, or miniscule flecks of color from wildflowers, which hardily defied the desolate conditions. From time to time, out of nowhere loomed a dramatically-sculpted, flat-topped rock formation, or an isolated bare peak, towering in striking contrast to the surrounding plain. Gorges and canyons were evidence of the historical presence of rushing water.

The train's windows were kept tightly shut despite the heat, to keep out the sand which was whipped up by the wind. I was fascinated by miniature, tornado-like spirals of sand and dirt, picked up by the hot air and spun into a whirling column. They mesmerized me, reminding me of Ellie Smith's tornado-borne journey to the Land of Oz, her adventures with her new-found friends, and her happy homecoming. These thoughts brought a lump to my throat, as I recalled Mikhail's parting words.

Mama was bad tempered, the boys were fractious, and I was weary from contemplating another readjustment and acclimation in a foreign land. Finally, after a boring but uneventful journey, we arrived at our destination, Leninabad, in northern Tajikistan.

Leninabad is a lively town, set in a deep river valley,

surrounded by majestic mountains that lay at the tail end of the Himalayan foothills. The location, so completely different from Siberia, is lush and colorful. The snow-capped peaks of the Pamir Mountains, rising towards Afghanistan in the distance, provide a breathtaking backdrop to the picture postcard panorama. The town lies on both sides of the Syr Darya River, and I have never before seen such stunning, turquoise blue-green water. From the moment we arrive my spirits are magically lifted by the beautiful tranquility of my surroundings.

I immediately set about doing some research to find out about our new home. I discover that Leninabad is an ancient town on the Silk Road from China to Europe, founded by Alexander the Great, and subsequently overrun by Arabs, then by Mongols under their leader Genghis Khan, and finally by the Russians. The Muslim presence is still very much in evidence; tall minarets puncture the skyline, while flocks of pigeons sunbathe on the mosques' colorful domes.

Papa is delighted to find that there is quite a large Jewish population, even though many of the town's original Jews have been driven away by Soviet religious oppression. Ironically, they've been replaced by an influx of refugees fleeing persecution in Europe.

The ever-organized Soviets have established a special school in town, where lessons are taught in both Russian and Polish. Unfortunately, as in the past, we have arrived in the middle of the school year, too late for me to enroll. Frustrated, I resign myself to a life similar to that of the past few years, of chores and babysitting. In Leninabad, however, things are different. Papa decides that I'm old enough to assist in his business.

He wastes no time in getting established, and soon he begins to make a profit, taking advantage of the policy of free trade in central Asia, where consumer goods are plentiful for those with money to purchase them. We have not seen such luxuries since leaving Tsanz four years ago. The first things Papa buys me are a new coat, shoes, and, wonder of wonders, a camera. I immediately embrace my new hobby of photography. There's certainly no shortage of fascinating subject matter to keep me occupied – portraits, points of interest, and panoramas abound. I become a regular visitor to the photography store in town, and soon I am accumulating a burgeoning collection of work. The store owner happily dishes out advice on techniques and composition, and even displays some of my photos in his window.

After several weeks, Papa announces one day that it's time to expand his business, and that he is looking further afield.

'Up in the hills above town there are some uranium mines, and a processing plant. They employ a large workforce, who will surely buy goods from me. Once I am organized, Tanya'leh, you will be my supplier.'

Papa enters into an agreement with the mine foreman, and travels up into the hills loaded with foodstuffs and, of course, candies. He sets up shop in a small cabin, and begins selling his goods to the laborers.

Every few days, I convey supplies to him, by hitching a ride on one of the trucks carrying ore to the processing plant. The ore is so heavy that it has to be packed into very small sacks, as anything larger can't be lifted. Once loaded, the trucks lumber slowly uphill, impeded by their cargo's weight. There's one particular spot above a bend in the road which makes an ideal springboard for me to jump with my packages onto the sacks.

I'm bursting with pride to have been recruited by Papa and entrusted with this responsibility. I relish the excitement of leaping on to the truck, and I imagine myself a traveling merchant-of-old, atop a caravan on the Silk Road, bringing wares to distant markets.

This routine lasts for a couple of months, and then I begin to notice that, on my arrival, several miners drift towards me offering to help me unload my packages and bring them to Papa. Papa, too, registers a surge in business on delivery days.

Soon my welcoming party has grown in size, its members competing openly, and quite aggressively, to assist me, until Papa has to intervene.

One day a few weeks later, I jump down from the truck alerted by a loud commotion at Papa's kiosk. Papa says a few harsh words, and the miners disperse. I ask him what all the fuss was about.

'Tanya'leh, I have decided to close the shop. I've made sufficient profit from the mine workers, so I can give up traveling to the hills and restrict my business to town.'

'But you are doing such profitable trade here. The men are almost fighting to be first in line. There must be another reason you want to quit.'

Papa has never been good at lying to me, and believes strongly in open honesty.

'The men are not fighting over my goods. They are fighting over *you*. They are bartering for you in true Tajik fashion, as if you are for a bride for sale. It's not safe for you to come here anymore. And I'm not sure about my own safety, if I keep refusing them.'

The decision is made and Papa stops travelling up to the mines. I'm anxious to find out what my new role will be in his business.

'I'm sorry, Tanya'leh, but in town I'll be able to manage without your assistance.'

I'm terribly disappointed that my employment is to be terminated, and beg him to find a different job for me to do. Anticipating my frustration, he quickly assures me.

'You won't be idle. I have engaged a tutor for you, so that you will be able to complete your final grade of school next year.'

In autumn, I enter the final grade in the Russian-Polish school. My classmates are intelligent and friendly, and we spend long hours into the night in serious discussion. There's a healthy mix of opinions on topics such as politics, religion, atheism, communism, and our plans for the future, should we ever be able to leave Leninabad. Many dream of attending university. I have always leaned towards art or theater, but having been exposed in recent years to so many different cultures, I wonder if perhaps anthropology might be a study option. My days are filled with studies and after school get-togethers. And my photography leads me along a continuous path to new discoveries around Leninabad.

My favorite place of all is the bazaar. After the monochromatic north, the sights, smells and sounds of the market are a heady, sensual feast. Everything about the place is exotic. Vendors hawk their wares in a cacophony of Tajik, Russian and even Polish, as well as other dialects I can't identify. Local women in brightly colored dresses and scarves carry live squawking chickens under their arms, while small children dart playfully between the legs of street performers, adding to the ruckus. Stalls heavily laden with all manner of fruits and vegetables, many of which I have never seen before, stand side by side with those offering bolts of brilliantly hued fabrics, sumptuous silks, and gaily patterned cottons. Hessian sacks filled with aromatic spices and all sorts of grains present a painter's palette of yellows, oranges, reds and browns. Rugs and housewares, baubles and trinkets, embroidered kaftans, fanciful headgear, and much more, entice buyers to part with their money after fierce negotiation.

The intricate artistry of the beautiful carpets, masterly woven in vibrant colors, reminds me of the ceiling in the Khodoriv synagogue, and I wonder whether the artist drew his inspiration from these Persian designs. Of all the bazaar has to offer, my preferred stop is the dried fruit stall, where I am honing my bargaining skills by haggling for figs, nuts and dates.

While I'm making friends of various nationalities and beliefs, Mama and Papa socialize mainly with other Jews. Apart from those who arrived from Eastern Europe, members of the town's Jewish community are mostly Bukharan, and it's intriguing to learn about their ways and customs, which are heavily influenced by Persian culture. Mouth-watering aromas are constantly emanating from our neighbor Mrs. Aminov's kitchen, and she takes pleasure in introducing me to traditional Bukharan foods. I'm addicted to a round flatbread called *lepeshka* which is baked in a special *tandyr* oven. Her cumin and turmeric spiced soup is hot, both in temperature and flavor, and several rice dishes are staples on her menu, such as *Plov*, slow-cooked rice with carrots and lamb, or *Baksh* which combines cubes of chicken with rice colored green by coriander.

'Why the sad face, Tanya?' she asked me the first time she served me *peraskhi*, fried pockets of dough stuffed with mashed potatoes and ground beef.

I described to her Grandfather's restaurant in Tsanz, and how he used to spoil me with freshly cooked *pierogi* and *pierniczki*. Even the names are almost the same. We still haven't received any word from home, and the worrying silence gnaws at me constantly.

On a happier note, one of Mrs. Aminov's four daughters recently got married. Bukharan Jews nearly always marry other Bukharan Jews, and marriages are traditionally arranged with the help of matchmakers. The groom's family pays a bride price, while the bride's family provides a large dowry. I was surprised to learn that Mrs. Aminov's daughter was only fourteen years old, but I was assured that in their community this was the normal age for a bride.

I was very excited to be invited to the wedding, which was no small affair. The celebrations, which lasted three days, included an inspection of the dowry payment and the bride price; a bridal shower at which an elderly aunt painted the bride's hands with henna; and the wedding ceremony itself. Mrs. Aminov explained that the wedding feast would include music and dancing, and she offered to teach me the traditional dances.

'You never know, Tanya. We may be able to find you a husband too.'

Considering my age, I feel that I'm already an old spinster in their eyes.

'I'm nineteen, Mrs. Aminov. I don't think I would fetch a very high bride price,' I laughed.

Accompanying me on a skin drum, she taught me all the dances, impressed by how quickly I picked up the steps and performed them.

'You know, Tanya, you could earn yourself some pocket money by dancing at weddings for a fee,' she suggested.

When the wedding day arrived, I felt as if I had fallen into a tale from *One Thousand and One Nights*, as I watched the bride, groom and wedding party enter, decked out in traditional kaftans and richly embroidered, fur-lined hats. I danced enthusiastically to the music, called *Shashmagam*, played by an ensemble of stringed instruments, moving as I had been taught to the Central Asian, Muslim-influenced rhythms. As I allowed the music to envelope me, I was overtaken by a feeling of release, of gay abandon, as if the nightmare experiences of the past few years were being sucked out of my body. Caught up in the pure joy of melody and movement, I lost any feelings of self-consciousness, oblivious to the people around me.

I must have performed well, as I am now commissioned to dance for payment by several families at their upcoming weddings. Mama is horrified at the thought of me dancing so publicly, and for money, 'like a wild gypsy', and insists that I stop. But I refuse to be denied this pleasurable and exciting opportunity, and I defy her.

Unfortunately, after several performances, it seems that my exposure to the wider community has resulted in a number of people suggesting matrimonial matches for me. Because of my age, all of the prospective grooms have at least one or more deficiencies, which preclude them from netting a younger girl. One particularly unattractive, balding specimen with buck teeth and questionable hygiene practices is having difficulty in accepting my refusal. None of the matches would appeal to me even if I was interested in marriage. But I'm not. My heart still belongs to Mikhail, even though his image is starting to fade in my memory.

Our sojourn in Leninabad is the happiest period I've known for a long time. Papa's business is flourishing, and we want for nothing. I enjoy school and have made many new friends. I write regularly to Erna, filling page after page with details of this fascinating place, in the hope that perhaps one of my letters might reach its destination, thousands of kilometers away. I never give up hope of receiving a reply, but she, like our family, remains ominously silent.

On the last day of school, the Principal calls me to his office to inform me that I've won a place at Leningrad University. Hardly able to grasp that finally one of my dreams is about to come true, I dash home, letter of acceptance in my hand, imagining the look of pride on Papa's and Mama's faces when I tell them the news. However, my balloon bursts the moment I open the door and see the expression on Papa's face. Stopped in my tracks, I hear him announce, 'The war is over. It's time to go home.'

'But Papa,' I protest, waving the letter at him. 'I have a place at Leningrad University.'

Papa's face lights up for a few seconds.

'Tanya'leh, this is wonderful news. You have done very well, and made me and your Mama very proud. But we have permission to leave and return to Poland right now. Who knows what Soviet policy will be, once the dust has settled? This may be just a small window of opportunity for us. We cannot afford to delay, and we have to be reunited with the family as soon as possible.'

Registering my look of disappointment, he takes hold of my hands and draws me towards him.

'I understand how much this university place means to you, but history shows that our people have never been treated well by the Russians, and the current policy of tolerance may well change overnight. You may find yourself expelled for being a Jew, before you even begin your studies.'

'But Papa, what about your original plan, to cross through Uzbekistan into Persia, and to make our way to Eretz Israel?'

'Tanya, it is a wonderful plan. But Mama and I know in our hearts that we can't abandon the family. And I'm certain you feel this way too. We have received no word from them for almost five years. I have decided. We have to go back to Poland to discover what has become of them.'

'But I have not forgotten my promise to you. One day, you will study at the Hebrew University in Jerusalem.'

On the day of our departure, Mrs. Aminov comes to say goodbye, armed with a large package of culinary delights for our journey. Some of my school friends and other well-wishers also turn up to see us off. Ever since news of the war's end reached Leninabad, there has been a steady stream of European exiles leaving the town, so while our neighbors are disappointed, they are not surprised to see us go.

Chapter 16

Return to Poland, 1945

We are on the last leg of our journey home, and my emotions helter-skelter between excitement and trepidation. Will everything be as I left it, or will Tsanz be unrecognizable? I begin to make mental lists of all the things I will do once we are home. First, I will shut myself in my old bedroom, absorb the sights and smells of my private sanctuary, and go one by one through all my possessions. Of course, now that I'm older I will probably discard some of them; perhaps Dovid would like to have the childish toys and books.

None of my old clothes will fit, so Mama and I will have to go into town and purchase a whole new wardrobe. I won't linger too long in the apartment, because I can't wait to see Erna. We have so much to talk about. I hope our friendship won't change now that we are young women, no longer little girls. But perhaps she is already married and has moved away. I refuse to dwell on unhappy scenarios.

I am deep in thought as our train crosses into the Ukraine. My musings are disturbed by quite a hubbub which erupts in the carriage. I look out of the window to see what the pointing and fuss is all about, and become an involuntary witness to the ravages of war; the countryside is littered with gutted houses, the charred remains of trucks and tanks, and rusty barbed wire. Death and destruction shroud the fields and villages, and I almost wish I was back in the closed cattle truck, from which I would not be able to see the sad scene through which we are passing.

And then the rumors of atrocities begin. We can't comprehend the scope of what has happened, until we are finally repatriated on Polish soil, and are confronted by some Poles.

'What are you doing here, Jews? We thought the Nazis had succeeded in murdering the lot of you. This is our country and we won't let you back in.'

Their voices drip with malice, their faces screwed up in disgust. The hatefulness of their words and grimaces hits me like a physical blow.

We have not heard anything from our family in Poland these past years. As we begin to grasp the enormity of the murder and destruction, we fear that the worst has befallen our nearest and dearest, and that we won't find anyone left alive.

'We will go to Tarnów first,' says Papa. 'Surely the family will have gathered there.'

Before we reach Tarnów, the train pulls in to the station of Ozwiecim. We ask where we are, and a railway worker points out a site in the distance.

'See that over there? That's the camp known as Auschwitz-Birkenau. The Nazis murdered millions of your people there.'

I think I must have misheard the man, or that he must be deranged to make such a ridiculously exaggerated statement. What can he mean by millions? I join a group of young fellow travelers who decide to go and see for themselves.

Climbing down from the train, I tell Mama and Papa not to worry about me.

'I'll meet up with you at the next station.'

My companions and I walk alongside a railway branch line through some fields for about twenty minutes, until we reach a gate, above which a decorative banner fashioned in wrought iron proclaims *Arbeit Macht Frei* (Work Makes You Free). The place is enormous, with row upon row of barracks, surrounded by layer upon layer of barbed wire fences and sinister watchtowers. At first glance it reminds me of the 'magical castle' we discovered in the taiga, and I give an involuntary shiver. We continue on a little further, and suddenly a most awful smell hits us.

'Cover your noses and mouths,' a worker shouts at us, 'to block out the scent of death. The smell and ash from the ovens still linger in the air.'

I am perplexed. 'Ovens?'

He comes over to us.

'First the bastards gassed the poor prisoners, and then cremated them.'

I feel physically sick, and put my hand over my mouth, fighting the urge to retch. I can see that my companions are reacting in the same way. One girl actually vomits, and another swoons.

We start to walk around the compound. The empty barracks bear witness to the suffering of those who had been incarcerated in them. Names and dates are scratched on the walls next to the tiers of wooden pallets, which are the only items of furniture. A stove stands alone in the center of the large space, and pieces of bloody rag and stains on the floor testify to violence, and unhygienic conditions.

We continue on to the far side of one of the barracks and peer inside what appears to be a storeroom. We stop dead in our tracks, as we are greeted by piles and piles of shoes; men's, women's and children's, in all sizes, styles and colors. In another storeroom there are piles of eyeglasses in every shape and form. There are mountains of battered suitcases with their owners' names chalked hopefully on the side, and heaps of human hair. Horror upon horror bombard us, much more than a young mind can absorb or process. It's incomprehensible. Surely no one is capable of doing this to other human beings.

I tremble in shock and anger, overwhelmed by what I am seeing. But the worst is yet to come. We make our way to one of the crematoria, a square brick building, whose tall chimney unremorsefully advertises its macabre function. With such an enormous task to complete, the workers have not yet managed to finish cleaning out the deep brick ovens. Some still contain skeletons, and the floor is scattered with bones. Tears course down my cheeks and sobs shake my whole body. I close my eyes and pray that none of my family or friends have met their death here.

Arm in arm, dumbstruck and horrified, lending each other support, my companions and I make our way back in grim silence to the train station. I climb on to the next available train to continue my journey.

How will I tell Papa what I have seen and heard? I don't believe there can be any Jews left alive in Poland. Perhaps 'millions' was no exaggeration at all. Other passengers are sharing the stories they have heard. How whole communities have been wiped out; ghettos, labor camps, forest massacres; more and more gruesome accounts. We describe what we have just seen in Auschwitz. People cry, rocking backwards and forwards.

One man holds his head in his hands, and wails, 'God has forsaken his people.'

Another cries, 'Why have we bothered to return to Poland if there is no one left?'

The atmosphere in the carriage is desolate, leaden with despair and despondency.

The train journey is slow with many stops. I eventually catch up with Mama and Papa at the third station, where our trains are now standing buffer to buffer. We continue on to Tarnów, avoiding conversation. I can't bring myself to describe to them what I have seen, and they don't share the horror stories they have heard.

At Tarnów, the station master informs us that the train will wait at the station for the entire day. Papa tells Mama to buy some refreshments and remain on the train with the boys until he returns.

'Come along with me, Tanya'leh,' he says, leading me off the train and out of the station.

The usual vibrant hustle and bustle of the station and its environs is etched in my memory from visits to my grandparents; the passing trams, cars and other vehicles, horse-drawn wagons, carts, and people milling around going about their business. Today, however, as we exit the station we may as well have stepped into a wilderness. A deafening silence greets us. I can't see even one miserable wagon. The entire town is stagnant. Solitary, downhearted people tread wearily on their way, almost in slow motion. I look around, and I'm not surprised. There is destruction everywhere.

Papa and I set out on foot in the direction of the Jewish quarter, stopping as we reach the corner of my grandparents' street. Or what I remember as their street.

'Are you sure this is the right place?' I ask Papa.

The Jewish quarter has disappeared. Zayde and Little Bubbe's building, like all the others, has been reduced to a pile of rubble. I rummage around in the dirt hoping to find something familiar, some keepsake, perhaps one of his beautiful watches, but there is nothing. Hundreds of years of history have been bombed and bulldozed.

We walk on, passing the tall building of the Talmud Torah, which has been spared, but lies empty and silent. And where are the happy voices of children in the Baron M. Hirsch School, which could always be heard in the street?

We carry on towards the corner of *ul. Żydowska* (Jewish Street), the place where the first Jews started to settle in the second half of the 15th century, and *Plac Rybny* (Fish Square), the site of the majestic Old Synagogue. How I loved to go there with Little Bubbe, to sit in the women's gallery and admire its opulent beauty. The synagogue was the pride of Tarnów, visible from afar to those approaching the city.

'Papa, we should be able to see it by now.'

In reply, Papa gasps. Instead of the magnificent building, we are faced by four blackened, damaged pillars upholding the stone *bimah,* the pulpit, from where the Rabbi used to read from the Torah every Sabbath and Holy Day. Apart from these remnants, the entire edifice has been destroyed.

Seeing our bewilderment, a passer-by comments that the Germans made a point of destroying all of Tarnów's synagogues.

'What happened to all the Jews?'

'Firstly, they were made to wear a special Star of David armband, and later they were herded into a ghetto. In 1942, some of them were taken to the cemetery and slaughtered there in a mass killing. Most of those who were still alive were shipped off to the Belzec concentration camp, and the rest to a second camp. Auschwitz I believe is its name.'

My knees buckle and Papa has to hold me up.

'Tanya'leh, what is it?'

Reluctantly, I tell him about the scenes I saw at Auschwitz, and we both weep.

Our hearts heavy, we turn northwards and walk for a further ten minutes, until we reach the Jewish cemetery. My Zayde once told me that the Tarnów cemetery was one of the largest and oldest Jewish cemeteries in all of Poland, with over four thousand graves. Some of the headstones were beautifully ornate, with inscriptions in Hebrew, Polish and German. As we approach we can see that the heavy iron entrance gate is still in place. Many of the gravestones are intact, although others have been desecrated. The entire area is overgrown with weeds and wild plants and is sadly neglected.

Papa covers his head, and in a trembling voice begins to recite *Kaddish*, the memorial prayer for the dead.

'Yisgadal v'yiskadash sh'mei rabo.' Glorified and sanctified be God's great name throughout the world.

I am relieved and comforted that Papa doesn't think, like the passenger on our train, that God has forsaken us.

When he has finished paying his respects to Tarnów's dead, Papa takes my hand, and deep in our own thoughts, we make our way back in solemn silence to the station. Now I realize that it's not surprising that the streets are so empty. That's what happens when half the town's population, the Jews, are wiped out, making the town *judenrein*, free of Jews.

Papa begins to describe to Mama what we have seen and heard, and I tell her a little of what I witnessed at Auschwitz.

'I have also heard some stories,' she tells us. 'Apparently, there was an uprising in the ghetto, led by the Jewish resistance. The Germans used airstrikes and canons to put down the revolt, destroying everything. We can't be sure that our family was taken to Auschwitz. There are witnesses who claim they perished in the ghetto uprising.'

Dead is dead, I think to myself, but perhaps at least they were spared the suffering and the indignity in the camps.

Chapter 17

Return to Nowy Sącz

The train continues its journey until we reach Silesia. I'm familiar with some of the area's history, because we learned about it in school. Control over this part of Poland alternated between Germany and Poland for many years, and sovereignty over the disputed region was a fierce bone of contention between the two. At the end of the First World War, the upper part of Silesia was allocated to Poland, while the Germans kept control of Lower Silesia. Upper Silesia was the first territory to be overrun by the Nazis at the outbreak of this war, claiming it back for Germany.

Having been recaptured by the Russians, Silesia is once again part of Poland, but the area is now divided into three sectors, American, British and Russian. We are told that the Silesian Germans have fled to the American sector, fearing reprisals for the Nazis' harsh treatment of the Poles during the war. Polish refugees returning from exile in areas under Russian control, like my family, are being settled in the Russian sector, in the empty houses the Germans have abandoned.

Much to our surprise we are allocated a magnificent house, which used to belong to a wealthy German, in the town of Jelenia Góra, previously known as Hirschberg in German. The house is filled with beautiful furniture and offers every creature comfort. The owners obviously fled in a hurry, leaving behind linens, towels, and dishes.

'Papa,' I whisper as we take in our new surroundings, 'I think we can forget the three-esses rule this time.'

Papa immediately finds work, and, once again, I have time on my hands. I set out to explore the town. Jelenia Góra enjoys a lovely setting, located in a fertile valley surrounded by thickly forested mountains. The entire area is well-known for its spas and thermal waters, reminding me of our summer vacations in Szczawnica. Luckily, the town appears to have escaped any significant damage during the war years.

I wander through the narrow, cobbled streets of Old Town to Town Hall Square, flanked by charming, colorful merchant houses and an impressive Town Hall. The air is clear and balmy, and the atmosphere in the square is tranquil. But suddenly I am covered in goosebumps, as it dawns on me that this place bears a strong resemblance to the square in Khodoriv, where Papa was forced to clean a Nazi tank. The hurtful memory comes flooding back, making my heart pump wildly as I recall the traumatic incident.

I consider sitting on one of the benches next to an elderly woman and a couple watching their two small children play in the square, but I'm held back by a feeling of uneasiness I can't quite explain. Is it my imagination or are they scowling at me? After all, they are Poles, who are no doubt angry to see a Jew back in their town. I hurry on, anxious to avoid confrontation.

After a couple of hours wandering the town, I return home.

'Where have you been?' Mama inquires.

'Just familiarizing myself with the town. It's really quite pleasant.'

'Well, don't get too fond of it, Tanya. I'm told that the city played host to part of the Gross-Rosen concentration camp, which claimed the lives of nearly 40,000, many of them Jews. I don't think we're going to enjoy a warm reception here.'

Papa is desperate to go to Tsanz, but has been advised that it would be extremely dangerous to do so. As soon as the Germans entered the city at the start of the war, the locals set upon the Jews, robbing them and taking over their properties. They happily informed on their neighbors to the Gestapo, and even took part in killings. So when a Jew returns to town trying to reclaim what is his, they beat him up and drive him away, or even worse. Nevertheless, I'm determined that if Papa decides to go I'm going with him.

Meanwhile, I have to look to the future. I can't just sit around twiddling my thumbs. I have talked to other refugees of my age, and several have decided that they are going to apply to university.

'There's a university in Wroclaw, a town not far from Jelenia Góra. We're going to register to study there. Why not come with us?'

Papa thinks it's a good idea.

'After all, Tanya'leh, you have your matriculation certificate with excellent grades, and the letter offering you a place at Leningrad University. You are bound to be accepted'

We take the train to Wroclaw, a large city on the banks of the River Oder, less than a hundred kilometers away. Before the war, the city was part of Germany and was known as Breslau. Leaving the central train station, we see destruction in every direction, testimony to the savage siege and hard fought Battle of Breslau, between the Nazis and the advancing Red Army, in the final months of the war. Rebuilding work is already well underway. I marvel at the arbitrary way in which one building stands unscathed, while its neighbor has been reduced to a heap of rubble. I'm reminded of the poor dead soldier who sheltered under the same tree as me during the Luftwaffe attack.

We catch a tram to the university, which overlooks the river. Many of its buildings have been damaged, and here, too, reconstruction is at fever pitch. On our way to the Admissions Office on the first floor of the main building, we pass the Aula Leopoldina, or Leopold Hall, a magnificent auditorium, decorated in the baroque style. The room's ornate beauty is breathtaking, and we pause to take in the sweeping painted ceiling, sculpted cherubs, marble pillars and rich frescoes.

After feasting our eyes on this stunning surprise, we present ourselves at the Admissions Office. One by one, we hand over our certificates to the registrar, and state the subjects we are interested to study; several of my companions wish to study medicine, another has chosen engineering, and I'm still interested in the arts. He looks over our papers and then gives a little nervous cough.

'You all have acceptable qualifications, but, unfortunately, you are Jews. The only subject you can study is philosophy. Nothing else is open to Jews here.'

He puts up his hand to quieten our protestations, and offers a possible solution.

'I recommend that the girls dye their hair blond and change their names to something not Jewish. Then there won't be a problem. There's nothing I can do for the boys'

I want to argue, but I can see it's pointless. Inside, I'm raging with anger, insult and frustration. Just along the corridor is one of the most beautiful rooms I have ever seen, while here is an office seething with ugliness. I hate the Poles more than ever. Anti-Semitism seems to flow in their veins, and the fate of the remaining Jews in Poland will never change. If I was in any doubt before, which I wasn't, now I'm certain that the sooner we leave Poland for Eretz Israel the better. I realize that Papa's prediction, that my place at Leningrad University would be jeopardized because of my religion, was well-founded, and I regret my anger at him.

When I get back from Wroclaw, I discover that Papa has

decided to risk the danger and travel to Tsanz.

'Perhaps I can find out what has happened to the family and salvage some of our belongings.'

I beg him to take me along but he refuses.

'Tanya'leh, I'm sorry, but it's too dangerous. I wouldn't be able to forgive myself if anything happened to you.'

He has forgotten that I'm not very good at taking no for an answer, and that once I make up my mind I won't budge. After all we have been through over the past few years, I reckon I've been in far more perilous situations. I accompany Papa to the train, and pretend to wave him off. Once he is settled inside, and the train starts to pull very slowly out of the station, I climb aboard a different carriage.

The journey takes much longer than I expected, and entails changing trains several times. I'm worried that Papa will spot me at one of the stations and send me back. My training with Magda in Przemyśl, in stealth, reconnaissance and smuggling, comes in handy, and I'm able to dodge in and out of trains without Papa noticing me.

At last, we are approaching the station in Nowy Sącz, which not so long ago I could see from our apartment window, and where I witnessed an innocent man shot down on the first day of war.

'Papa,' I call out, as I follow him out of the station. He turns, and I can see he is furious with me for disobeying him, but I sense that his anger is tempered with a little relief in not having to face this alone. After he finishes reprimanding me, he takes my arm and warns me not to move from his side.

'We won't be wandering around here as we did in Tarnów. We must keep a low profile, and just focus on what we came for.'

At first glance, Tsanz seems the same as when we left it

to begin our exile, but to me it feels completely different. Or perhaps I was so familiar with it then, that I didn't notice what was rumbling underneath the surface. As in Tarnów, we find that here, too, the city is *judenrein*. The Old Synagogue is miraculously still intact, but the cemetery has been decimated, and, to my disgust, I see that the road up the hill leading to my school is paved with Jewish gravestones.

We make our way to our old apartment. Papa asks to be let in but we are turned away.

'Get out of here, dirty Jews,' shouts the man who has stolen our home.

As we move away I hear a familiar whinnying from the stable next door. I peek in and see my two old friends, Tancerz and Shaynan, looking much wearier and thinner than when I left them. Tancerz nuzzles me gently.

'I'm so sorry,' I sob, stroking his soft nose, 'I don't have an apple for you today.'

Papa pulls me away. 'Come, Tanya.'

I get a lump in my throat as we pass by Erna's building, and, hopefully, I lift my eyes up to the second floor, but they are met by the hostile gaze of a stranger looking down on us from a window in her apartment. We hurry on to Papa's gentile friend Karol. His face lights up when he opens his door and sees Papa. He hugs him tightly.

'Thank goodness you have survived, my friend. You are luckier than most.'

While we sit in his living room drinking tea, Karol tells Papa that he managed to save our valuables from the basement.

'But my brother-in-law told me that if you ever came back to claim them, he would not let me return them to you. My brother-in-law is a pig, excuse me Tanya, and he is also a violent man. I fear not only for myself, but for you too. Nevertheless, I'll give you what I can.'

Leaving me safely in his apartment, Karol takes Papa to his old candy factory, which no longer bears the Anglische name, and helps him load some small pieces of machinery and equipment onto a cart. They come back for me, and then Karol helps us make our way back to the station with our loot.

'I regret I can't help you more,' says Karol to Papa, secretly slipping him a handful of money.

'Goodbye and good luck, my friend.'

On our journey home, Papa repeats to me what Karol has told him about the fate of Mama's family. When the Nazis began their 'selections', Grandmother suffered a heart attack and died. My darling Grandfather was taken to Auschwitz, with my aunt Shoshana and her two small children. Karol told Papa that he went to Shoshana and begged her to let him hide the two girls, or take them to a convent, but she refused saying, 'whatever our fate, my girls and I will face it together.' Another aunt fled to Tarnów, but died there in the ghetto. One of my uncles escaped to the Ukraine, but he and his wife were brutally murdered there. Karol did not know what happened to the rest of Mama's siblings.

'Tanya'leh,' says Papa after a short silence. 'You won't believe the name of the commandant of the city, and overseer of the Jewish liquidation. It's Hamann.'

Papa spits as he says the name. '*SS-Obersturmführer* Heinrich Hamann, from the Gestapo. He killed dozens of Jews with his own hands, and shipped the rest off to death camps.'

I am stunned. Surely this is no coincidence. It's the same name as the evil Haman, who we remember on Purim, my favorite Jewish holiday. Haman, in the story recounted in the Book of Esther, was a vizier in the court of the Persian King

Ahasuerus. He hatched a plot to kill all the Jews throughout the Persian Empire, but his evil intentions were foiled by Queen Esther, herself a Jew.

In Rabbinical tradition, Haman is considered to be the archetype of evil and persecutor of the Jews. How hideously fitting that the murderer of Tsanz's Jews shares his cursed name.

Chapter 18

Time to Move Forward, 1946

It's clear that we should get out of Poland as soon as possible. Papa not only fears for our survival as Jews among people who despise us, but also dreads life under the communist regime. We have lived under Soviet rule long enough to know that we must take the first opportunity to put it far behind us.

I have heard that groups of young people have joined a movement called *the Zionist Youth*. They come from the remnant of Europe's Jewish children; survivors from the death camps, those who were hidden in convents, farms, and villages, and others who fought alongside the partisans. Their plan is to make their way to Eretz Israel, by somehow running the British blockade. I hurry to join, hoping against all hope that my dearest Erna has survived and is amongst them. Sadly she isn't.

The group I join numbers about forty, and we plan to escape from Poland illegally, as soon as we are given the green light by the movement's leaders. We will cross the border into Czechoslovakia, continue to Austria, and then to Germany. From there we will have to make our way to the coast, either through France or Italy, to await illegal transportation to our destination. While the plan is fraught with difficulties, initially the group's biggest obstacle is lack of funds. So we are sent to look for work.

By now I have a long resume of past experience; wood gathering, grave digging, cotton picking, water hauling, latrine cleaning, none of which I'm anxious to repeat. Luckily, out of everyone in the group I'm the most educated, and I speak several languages, so I land myself a position in one of the town's municipal offices, overseeing a staff of fifty Germans. They are all old men. It seems that all the young employees have run away to Germany.

It's my job to distribute and explain assignments, to translate from Polish to German, and tell them what to do. Who could possibly have imagined the surreal picture of a bunch of elderly Germans bowing and scraping to a young Jewish woman, a survivor of their countrymen's brutality? I hate the job and, despite the irony, I take no pleasure in their humiliation, as they address me, *'ja Fraulein, nein Fraulein, bitte Fraulein'* (yes Miss, no Miss, please Miss).

My wages are good, compared to those of my friends, who are employed mostly in odd jobs and manual labor. Between us we are making a significant contribution to the group's kitty, which will be used to sustain us until we are ready to leave, and then to bribe our way across borders.

The work is boring and my nerves are taut, impatient for the signal to be on our way. Finally, after several weeks, the order comes; tonight we will cross the border. Mama tries to dissuade me from leaving, but Papa knows that once I have made up my mind there will be no changing it.

'If you must go, I want you to take Jozef with you.'

I don't want to be saddled with my brother. He's older now, and no longer needs me to tell him fairy tales, but it's still a burden and responsibility I would rather not have.

'But Mama, it will be risky enough for me, without having to worry about someone else.'

'Tanya'leh,' says Papa, 'we have stuck together no matter what, until now. This is the first time we will be separated, and who knows if or when we will meet up again. At least you will have a brother, you won't be alone.'

We are warned that we won't be allowed to carry any bags, so I put on as many clothes as I can, just like I did when we first ran away from Tsanz. Mama gives me a few remaining pieces of jewelry, and I take my treasured Leica camera. After a tearful goodbye, Jozef and I leave to join the group. It turns out that other families have made a similar decision, and four more siblings are to escape with us.

We head out of town in a south-easterly direction, towards the border with Czechoslovakia. Our path takes us through woods up into the hills, and as I climb, and the temperature drops, I'm very glad of my layers of clothing. The uphill path is strenuous, and scattered with boulders, loose stones and fallen branches, which trip us up in the dark. Jozef falls and scrapes his knees but, to my surprise, he soldiers on bravely without complaint.

We walk in silence for hours, taking only short breaks to wait for stragglers to catch up. Eventually, we reach the border crossing, marked by a small hut, a searchlight, and two armed guards with a vicious-looking dog. I'm not the only one in the group experiencing déjà vu, and raw fear is etched on the faces of many.

The guards look us over threateningly, but make no real effort to prevent our leaving.

'Go, Jews, and good riddance,' they growl at us.

But as we pass they search us, one by one, and confiscate our valuables. Luckily, I have hidden Mama's jewelry in my underwear, but one of the guards greedily wrenches my precious Leica from my hands. I'm devastated, but if this is the price of freedom, so be it.

There don't appear to be any guards on the Czech side, and

we safely make our way to a pre-arranged meeting point, where food and water await us. We are welcomed by two operatives of the *Bricha* (Escape) movement, which manages a network of routes and transit camps across Europe, smuggling survivors out of Europe to Eretz Israel.

'You may rest here for a couple of days. From here we have a long trek to the German border, and you will need all your strength.'

I grab a couple of blankets, one for me and one for my brother.

'Come on, then, Jozef. Let's have a look at those knees and get them cleaned up.'

Three days later, we cross from the Czech to the German side of the border, where we are met by trucks, which take us to the outskirts of Munich, to a camp called Reithofen.

'Look over there, Jozef,' I say pointing at a sign, *UNRRA*, stenciled in large black letters on the side of some wooden crates.

'We must be in the American Sector.'

For the first time in years, I feel excited and optimistic that there's a future to look forward to.

Chapter 19

Down on the Farm

The camp is not really a camp at all. It's called a *kibbutz*, an agricultural training farm, where special instructors will prepare us for the pioneering life we'll encounter in Eretz Israel. Unlike most of the group members, I had a Zionist upbringing and education, and have dreamed for a long time of immigrating to the Jewish homeland. For many others, however, the whole concept is entirely new.

We are greeted by Shmuel, who comes from an actual Israeli kibbutz. He describes his life there, with a sparkle in his eyes, and a tremble of emotion in his voice, infusing everyone with his enthusiasm and pioneering spirit.

In addition to fairly Spartan living quarters, the farm complex boasts a large cowshed, stables, and pens for other animals, outhouses, a garage, and several empty buildings. Open fields as far as the eye can see are cultivated with a variety of crops, wheat and grains, and vegetables. It's rumored that the property once belonged to Hitler's family. It pleases me to think that it's now part of the rehabilitation project which will give young Jews a new life.

Our original group has expanded, and we now number ninety – five girls and the rest boys. Most of the boys are sent to work in the fields, or to learn engine maintenance in the garage, but Jozef, being one of the youngest, is allocated to the stables.

'Tanya, I'm scared of horses,' he complains when he finds out that he is to be a groom.

I try to encourage him.

'Scared? Don't you remember Tancerz and Shaynan, our neighbors in Nowy Sącz? They are the friendliest creatures in the world. I'm so jealous of you. I'd love to swap my job with yours.'

With the rest of the girls, and a few boys, I'm sent to work in the cowshed. The strong smell of manure is overpowering, far less pleasant than the horse pooh that Jozef will have to deal with. Our first job is learning to milk the cows. Our instructor, Hans, is a German who worked on the farm before the Americans confiscated it. He makes fun of us, and names the cows after the girls in the group.

'This one,' he announces, 'is Sonia. And this is Miriam,' he continues, pointing to a particularly large cow. The girl Miriam is quite large herself, and isn't amused by his choice of namesake.

Hans sits down on a low three-legged stool, which he has positioned towards the cow's rear end, and demonstrates how to get the udders to release their milk. At the end of the demonstration he surveys the group and asks, 'Who wants to go first?'

Without waiting for a volunteer he calls on me.

'How about you, Tanya?'

I sit down nervously on the stool. Surely it can't be that different from milking Wanda, the goat I practiced on during our summer vacation in Szczawnica. Another skill I never thought I'd have occasion to use. It only takes me a couple of tries to get the milk flowing.

'Beginner's luck,' says Hans, surprised by my dexterity, and he grudgingly congratulates me.

Encouraged by my success, Miriam steps up to have a go. Unfortunately, she doesn't have my past experience, and tugs violently at her namesake's udders, which just aggravates the cow and makes her stubborn. Hans laughs heartily, and the others giggle, but they don't fare any better when it's their turn. By the end of the day, we are exhausted, but have mastered the finer points of milking.

Jozef and I exchange stories of our first day's work, and I'm glad to hear that, after his initial reluctance, he's actually happy in the stables. His duties include cleaning out the stalls, shoveling hay, and washing and brushing the horses, and he says he finds the work invigorating.

As days go by, I begin to see how being close to nature and undertaking physical work has a therapeutic, restorative effect on my workmates, who for so long were subjected to the soul-destroying inactivity of prison life, and how it helps to rebuild their sense of self-worth. They are motivated and have a sense of purpose, bringing with it the first sparks of hope for the future.

Having mastered the art of milking, we learn how to make butter and cheese. My thoughts return to my friend Ola in Nizhneudinsk, and the freshest butter I ever tasted, churned by her mother from their pet cow's milk.

'Today,' announces Hans, 'you will become midwives. Sonia is in labor, and you will have to help her deliver her calf.'

We all look from one to another in astonishment. Under Hans's direction, the boys hold Sonia's head still, talking to her softly and reassuring her, while we girls have the privilege of taking turns in thrusting an arm deep within the cow, grabbing a small leg, and helping to ease the calf's way out into the world. From the squeamish point of view, this is marginally better than my experience of watching surgeons operate on a wounded soldier; but the hygiene leaves a lot to be desired, and since the cow is not under anesthetic, she is much less cooperative than the unconscious patient. When it's over, we all marvel in wonderment at the miracle of new life. How symbolic!

The next morning, Shmuel approaches me.

'Tanya, I understand that you speak Hebrew. One of the highest priorities in the kibbutz movement is to teach Hebrew. A shared language will help to bridge the gap between the different nationalities, and smooth their transition into their new life.'

And so begins my career as a teacher.

Every morning, I get up at dawn and go to work with the others. When we finish our assignments, we change out of our stinking work clothes, and my class begins. Everyone is very tired, but my students are anxious to learn. They have been robbed of six years of schooling, and understand the importance of making up for the lost time. Even my brother Jozef has not attended school regularly since we left Nowy Sącz, and is far behind in his education.

It's a difficult task, but it gives me satisfaction and purpose. There are no textbooks, no blackboard or chalk, and paper and pencils are scarce. Students range in age from eight to eighteen. Those who were too young to have attended school before the war have only rudimentary skills, and many don't know how to read and write, particularly the youngest among them. Their classmates, who would be graduating high school now if the Nazis had not cut short their education, have a lot to catch up on.

And there are those who have deep, psychological scars, and are haunted by their experiences. A sudden outburst often unnerves the class and disrupts the students' concentration. One boy suffers from what the doctor calls *'fits of hysteria'*. Out of nowhere, without any warning signs, he loses consciousness, and then begins to thrash about, screaming and shouting about the awful things that happened to him. We can do nothing except sit with him, calm him down, and protect him from doing himself harm.

Others have deep, physical scars. One boy was hidden by a farmer in a dovecote. His protector brought him food, but he was not allowed to come out for fear of discovery. He spent so much time in the small narrow space that he became bent like a little old man, a hunchback. He has straightened up now, but every so often he has some kind of seizure; he folds himself over again, and sits completely still and silent.

Children who survived the concentration camps have a need to tell their stories. And who do they tell them to? To me. They call me '*the normal one*', because I wasn't in the camps, and I still have a family. If I have learned one thing from my experiences over the past few years, it's that everything is relative. I am, indeed, the lucky one. Despite the hardships I have endured, Fate could have dealt me a much harsher blow. Most of them have no-one; they are alone in the world.

They tell me about unimaginable atrocities, and this narration seems to help them achieve emancipation from the past. Their accounts weigh heavily on my heart, and I have to try hard not to dwell on them.

One boy, Pinchas, comes from my home town. He has only one leg. He survived Auschwitz, but just before the camp was liberated, a German soldier shot him in the leg with a poisoned bullet. The Americans took him to hospital, where surgeons had to amputate in order to save his life. He is a handsome fellow, tall and blond, but he despises himself and everyone around him.

Pinchas is an exceptionally talented artist, and has painted stunning murals on the walls of our living quarters. It's simultaneously amazing and disconcerting to watch the way he paints frantically, in a frenzy of anger. Perhaps, when he reaches Eretz Israel, he will be able to channel all that wild energy, and become a successful artist.

The days pass by swiftly, but after a year on the kibbutz, I decide the time has come to move on. I feel that I have begun to tread water, and that I'm no nearer to reaching Eretz Israel.

Another problem is the boy to girl ratio on the farm, which is eighty-five to five. The boys seem to think that there are no more eligible females left in the world, so they keep proposing marriage to me and the other four girls. It's like being back in Tajikistan but worse. Marriage is the last thing on my mind. I've stopped pining for Mikhail, in fact I haven't thought about him at all in a long while, but that doesn't mean that I'm willing to settle for a match of convenience devoid of the passion in Erna's novels. I am determined to wait for '*the one*'.

The boys pester me all the time. Jozef can see that it bothers me, and has begun acting like my chaperone, deflecting my suitors' attentions. But it's so uncomfortable and unpleasant to keep saying 'no', and I can see that the problem is not going to go away. So it seems that the solution is for me to go away instead.

Chapter 20

Displaced Person

I have decided to take the train to a nearby displaced persons camp, Leipheim, where I've discovered Mama's youngest sister, Esther, is living. I long to see a familiar face, and perhaps she will have some news of Mama and Papa's whereabouts. They must have left Jelenia Góra, and I have lost contact with them. In DP camps, lists of survivors' names are circulated and efforts are made to trace lost relatives, so Esther may know where they are.

I throw a little farewell party for my students, encouraging them to continue with their studies, and wishing them well for the future. I'm reminded of the end-of-school graduation party in Tsanz, and reiterate poor Mr. Koplinsky's blessing, that we should all meet up in Eretz Israel. He, and all my schoolmates save three, didn't survive.

Jozef understands that I can't take him with me. I have no concrete plans as yet, and he will be better off staying on the kibbutz with his new friends and a job he likes, rather than traipsing around from place to place with me. I promise to send for him as soon as I am settled or have located our parents.

Shmuel is unhappy to see me leave, but doesn't try to persuade me to stay. He even gives me a ride to the nearest railway station. The train doesn't go directly to Leipheim, and I have to change at Munich.

The contrast between the quiet, pastoral ambience of farm life, and the chaotic hubbub at Munich station is dramatic. The Americans have made train travel free in their zone, and it feels like the entire population of Germany is on the move, taking advantage of this generosity.

The station is packed and noisy, the air thick with the acrid smell of train engines, smoke, and human odor. I have to push and shove my way between platforms, navigating a surging mass of would-be passengers, and those recently disgorged from arriving trains. It's quite a terrifying experience for someone of my small stature, and it takes every ounce of my strength and determination to avoid being swept away in the wrong direction or, worse still, crushed.

A cacophony of shouting, garbled loudspeaker announcements, and screeching train wheels, adds to the pandemonium. I finally find a seat on the right train, and slump down exhausted and disheveled.

The Leipheim Displaced Persons Camp is a sprawling complex, just a short walk from the station. As soon as I arrive I go looking for Esther, Mama's youngest sister. I haven't seen my aunt for nearly eight years, and I'm now the same age she was when I left home. Our reunion is not as joyful as I expected. Esther briefly shares her experiences with me.

'I escaped from Tsanz with several friends, but we were caught by the Russians and sent to a labor camp.'

She introduces me to her husband, Eli, one of her fellow Tsanz escapees, whom she married in the labor camp, and they proudly show off their sweet baby boy.

'Eli's work in the camp was back-breaking, and he became very weak. After the baby was born, he decided that we had to try to escape. One night, a fire broke out in the camp, and while the guards' attention was distracted we slipped away.'

Somehow they managed to survive living rough for many months, and to make their way back to Poland.

'It was clear that even though the war was over we weren't safe there, so we continued to travel west with a group of refugees, and we ended up here.'

Of course, she is relieved to learn that Mama and the rest of us survived, but the reception I receive from her is not particularly warm or encouraging.

'Look, Tanya,' she says, rather unpleasantly, 'we have only one room and the food here is rationed. I can't share my meal ticket with you. You won't be able to get your own one because you have no papers, and don't really belong here.'

I choose to put her meanness down to the deprivations she has suffered, even though I remember that she always was a mean-spirited girl, much like her mother, my grandmother.

'I tell you what,' she continues. 'There are lots of bachelors here, and I'm sure I can find you a good match. As a married woman you will get a room and be entitled to share your husband's ration card.'

First Tajikistan, then the kibbutz, and now here! Is getting married the only thing people think about, I wonder to myself? After a day or two in the camp, I realize that, yes, it's certainly the case here.

A camp instructor explains to me that most of the survivors have lost their entire families, and one of the most vivid expressions of their will to live is to build new ones. On my first day at the camp I witness no less than five weddings, and I marvel at the number of women pushing baby carriages. Nevertheless, I'm furious with Esther's suggested solution to my problems.

The Leipheim camp is very well organized. There is a kindergarten, an elementary school, and a vocational school; a Talmud Torah school and a yeshiva have also been established.

There is a library, and even a soccer club, *Makabi Leipheim*. Some of the residents produce and circulate a newspaper, *A Heim* (A Home); others have formed a theater group, and there are lots of cultural activities.

What the camp doesn't provide, however, are employment opportunities. This fact, added to my aunt's lack of enthusiasm at my presence, plus her matchmaking efforts to find me a *shidduch*, a husband, propels me to move on again. I make some enquiries, and discover that there is another camp not too far away where residents are allowed, and even encouraged, to work. Having made my decision, I go to tell Esther my plans.

'Goodbye, aunt. If you hear from Mama, please let her know where I am.'

It's lunchtime when I arrive at my destination, and after a few questions, the welcoming official points me in the direction of the dining hall.

'Get yourself something to eat, Miss Anglische,' he says, handing me a coupon, 'and then come back, and we'll organize your sleeping arrangements, and see what work we can find for you to do.'

I think Papa would be proud that I'm independently continuing to follow his three-esses rule. The dining hall is crowded and noisy, and a long line has formed at the food counter. While I wait I scan the large room. Half way around I stop dead in my tracks, hardly able to believe my eyes. Am I dreaming? I look more closely. No, it really is Luba, a classmate from the school in Siberia.

People around me are taken aback to see me jumping up and down and waving frantically, shouting out her name, hoping to be heard above the noise. They probably think I'm having some sort of fit. But at least I catch Luba's attention and she looks my way, a huge grin spreading across her face. We run into each other's arms, half laughing, half crying, both talking at once.

'Tanya,' says Luba's mother, 'How wonderful to see you. Are your parents and brothers with you?'

I explain as briefly as I can where I have been since leaving Siberia.

'Unfortunately, I have lost contact with my parents, but I hope I'll be able to track them down while I'm here.'

Unlike my aunt, Luba's parents welcome me warmly, offering to share what little they have.

'Thank you, but I intend to find a job, so I will be able to afford my own meal tickets.'

I can't believe my luck. I have been offered a job in the UNRRA administration office, which pays a small salary. I have my own room and my own food coupons. At last, I don't have to accept charity, and it's a wonderful, emancipating feeling. I cherish my sense of independence and self-determination.

Now that I'm settled, I decide it's time to bring Jozef to live with me here. I have no idea who, if anyone, has been taking classes since I left the kibbutz, and there is a good school here for him. I have also decided to write to an uncle, one of Mama's brothers, who, according to Esther, escaped from Tsanz to Eretz Israel. The problem is I don't know where he is exactly.

There is an instructor, Daniel, who has been sent from Eretz Israel to work in the camp, and when I approach him with my problem, he kindly offers to help me track down my uncle's address. Daniel is very impressed that I can speak Hebrew.

'Your knowledge of the language is a rare commodity, Tanya. Why don't you teach in the school? You have no idea how desperate we are for people like you.'

'But I like my job,' I protest, omitting to tell him that, although I have some teaching experience, I prefer the administrative work I'm doing now. Refusing to give in so quickly, Daniel suggests enrolling me on a crash course.

'Then you can decide.'

Reluctantly, I agree.

The course only lasts a few days, during which time I meet several emissaries from Eretz Israel, each of whom tries to convince me to work in the school.

'Tanya, you have no idea how important this work is. It's a real *mitzvah* (good deed). Many of the children were hidden and raised by Christians, or secluded in monasteries and convents. They do not know what it is to be Jewish. Your responsibilities will be twofold; not only to teach them the language, but also to reacquaint them with their heritage. They desperately need to gain a sense of belonging and community.'

Actually, I have firsthand knowledge of what they mean. While I was in Jelenia Góra, our Zionist Youth group was sent out on several missions to look for such 'Christianized' children. Persuading nuns to relinquish their charges was not an easy task, and some of the children secluded in isolated villages did not want to leave their Christian 'families', frightened of losing 'parents and siblings' all over again. While teaching on the kibbutz I was reunited with one of the children we had rescued in Poland. Her fellow *kibbutzniks* became her new family.

By the end of the teaching course, the pull at my heart strings, and at my conscience, supersedes my desire to stay in my office job, and I agree to become a teacher once again.

Teaching is no easier here than it was on the farm. I am faced with illiteracy, concentration and behavior issues, and a dire lack of textbooks, stationery and other learning materials. At least language is not a problem. The one thing for which I thank my exile is my command of Ukrainian, Russian and Yiddish; I can communicate with the children in all of these languages, and, of course in Polish and Hebrew. I also understand quite a lot of German, and I have even picked up a few English words during my short stint in the UNRRA office.

One morning, after managing as best I can for several weeks, a colleague bursts into my classroom flushed with excitement.

'Tanya, come and look. An organization called the Joint Distribution Committee has sent us piles of text books, pencils, and notebooks.'

By the level of rejoicing one might have thought we'd struck gold. The delivery is indeed a real treasure, and is a great morale booster for teachers and students alike. It's heartwarming to see each of the students' faces light up with pride when they are presented with their very own set of learning materials.

After three months of teaching, I still have had no contact with my parents. Jozef has settled in at the camp and in school, but he misses the rest of the family. Daniel still has no news about the whereabouts of my uncle, and I have just about given up hope of ever hearing from him.

Several of the new friends I have made in the camp, some of whom are from Eretz Israel, are working for the *Bricha* movement, smuggling people across the Austrian-German border. I hint to Daniel that I'm interested in volunteering, and after a couple of weeks, he secures permission for me to take part in the operation. I am paired with another operative, Shlomo, who already has *Bricha* experience.

'First we reconnoiter the escape route,' he instructs me. 'Sometimes it's across a river, or through a forest. We wait for a very dark or rainy night, and then we cross over to the Austrian side.'

Following his direction, a few days later I find myself huddled in a damp forest, waiting to receive a group of escapees.

'It's imperative that we keep them completely quiet, Tanya. If we get caught retracing our steps back into Germany, not only will we all get sent back to the Austrian side, but we will also be jeopardizing future operations, since the border guards will discover the routes we are taking.'

Leading my charges in a line behind me, I feel like the Pied Piper of Hamelin. Of course, my clothes are black rather than brightly colored, and I don't play a pipe to lure them away. Rather, we all move along solemnly, keeping low in complete silence.

One afternoon, Daniel greets me outside my classroom, grinning from ear to ear and waving a letter at me.

'Here you are, Tanya. From Eretz Israel.'

I don't know how he managed it, but his contacts at home found my uncle, and passed my letter on to him. In his reply, Uncle writes that he has been in contact with Mama and Papa. As soon as they could leave Poland legally, they made their way into Austria, and are in a camp in a place called Steyr.

I hug Daniel '*thank you*', and run to my room to write to them at once.

Shortly before the next escape operation, I receive Papa's reply, begging me and Jozef to join the family in Steyr. Shlomo consults with our Bricha superiors.

'Complete this last mission, Tanya, and then, on the next operation, you can take your brother with you, and remain on the Austrian side, instead of returning to Germany. It will be up to you to find your own way to Steyr.'

We set out on what is to be my last mission. To date, Shlomo and I have made three nerve-wracking excursions, and, so far, we have been lucky. It's chilly and rainy, and Shlomo decides that we will use a route through the forest rather than risk additional wetness and cold by crossing the river. We rendezvous with our counterparts on the Austrian side, and take charge of our consignment of refugees.

There are a large number of children in the group, and

keeping them quiet is difficult. Suddenly, we hear shouts of 'Achtung', and, according to procedure, Shlomo and I split up, each taking half of the group in a different direction.

I can't risk getting caught. What will happen to Jozef, left behind in Germany, if I don't come back for him? Shlomo must be having similar thoughts, and bravely he lures the German border guards away from my position. Confident that Shlomo will be able to handle the situation, I hurry my charges away under cover of the forest, until we are well inside Germany.

When I get back to camp I report the incident to Daniel.

'I'm so grateful to Shlomo, but am worried for his safety, which he risked on my behalf. Please try to find out what has happened.'

Daniel promises to make inquiries, and a few days later word reaches us that Shlomo is safe.

Chapter 21

Reunion

Today I said a tearful goodbye to Luba and her family.

'Next year in Jerusalem,' we promised each other.

Jozef and I gathered up our belongings, and set out on our way to Austria.

The crossing is uneventful, and I'm delighted to see Shlomo waiting on the other side, ready to take a new group into Germany. We hug, and I mouth a silent thank you to him, as we part.

I have some money, but we have no papers, and I'm terrified that I will be asked to present them before we reach Steyr. As it turns out, a lot of people appear to be moving around without the necessary documentation, and we are free to travel by train without them.

Tears and laughter intermingle in an emotional reunion with Mama and Papa. Little Dovid seems to have doubled in size since I last saw him.

It doesn't take long, however, before Mama expresses her displeasure with my appearance.

'Tanya, you look more like a boy than a girl, with your shirt and trousers, and your hair pulled back in a most unattractive fashion.'

Intent on restoring my femininity, she finds me a dress from somewhere, and insists on me wearing lipstick. Really, lipstick!

'There is a decent hairdresser here. Perhaps she can do something with you.'

I suppose I shouldn't be shocked or surprised that, in these difficult times, she sets store by such inconsequential trivialities. After all, what can one expect from a woman who insisted on wearing stiletto heels when she was running away from the Nazis? No doubt, her next mission will be matchmaking, seeking out a *shidduch* for me.

The residents in the Steyr camp live in barracks, which formerly housed German troops. They receive food coupons, which they exchange for bread, and queue in long lines for their lunchtime meal. Having enjoyed self-sufficiency for more than a year, I can't bear the thought of accepting handouts again. On the kibbutz I worked hard for my room and board. While I worked for UNRRA I received a salary, and ate in their cafeteria. I'm not prepared to go back to living on charity, so I'll have to find some employment.

Next door to Mama and Papa lives the principal of the camp school, Mr. Klingman. As soon as my parents arrived in Steyr the two families immediately struck up a friendship, and when Mr. Klingman learned that Papa had some managerial experience, he appointed him school administrator.

Today, knowing that I'm looking for work, Mr. Klingman approached me with a suggestion.

'Tomorrow a special emissary is coming to Steyr. His mission is to collect the children, and take them to a sort of summer camp near the lakes, to restore their health and well-being. Let me introduce you to him. Perhaps he can find you a job.'

The following afternoon a jeep pulls into the camp. Out steps a tall, good looking, but noticeably overweight man, dressed in the uniform of an American officer. I assume he must be important, since he has his own driver to ferry him about, which is an unusual sight indeed. He is sporting the standard US soldier crewcut, 'short back and sides'. I can't help turning up my nose when I notice that he is smoking one cigarette after another.

Mr. Klingman greets him, and together with the school administrator, Papa, they sit down to iron out the arrangements for the summer camp.

I can just about overhear them and am surprised that the conversation is being conducted in Hebrew.

'We have a lot of children, from this camp and from others,' says the visitor, 'but we have very few counsellors and almost no educators. Perhaps you can find me some volunteers here, who are willing to come along as instructors and teachers.'

'You are in luck, Aaron,' beams Klingman.

'Just a few days ago, a young woman, my administrator's daughter in fact, arrived at the camp. She has teaching experience and even speaks Hebrew,' he adds, pointing in my direction and waving me over.

'Tanya, this is our special emissary, Aaron Freed.'

I'm amazed to discover that he's not an American at all. He's from Eretz Israel, an undercover agent of sorts.

Klingman outlines what has been discussed, and asks if I'm willing to help. Of course, I agree immediately. Anything is better than sitting around here with nothing to occupy me.

Mama is horrified when Papa tells her that I'm leaving again.

'But you just arrived,' she complains. 'Why are you in such a hurry to leave?'

I explain that I have to do something useful, something positive, that will help the poor children.

'Jozef will stay with you, and you'll hardly notice I'm not here,' I add in an attempt to appease her.

Aaron explains that there will be two camps, one for religious children, and one for secular children.

'The daily educational and activities program will be suited to the needs of the participants.'

The arrangements are finalized in a matter of hours, and next morning I find myself on a train with the children to an unknown destination. Aaron informs me that I will be working in the religious camp.

'I have great respect for religion, but I haven't practiced it for many years. I won't know what to do,' I tell him, certain that he has made the wrong decision.

'Not to worry,' he assures me, rather offhandedly. 'I'm sure you will cope.'

The train journey takes us into the beautiful Austrian countryside. Lush green meadows and rolling hills are dotted with small villages and pretty farmhouses, and further in the distance, snow-capped Alpine peaks survey the scene from their majestic height. How is it possible, I wonder, that such beauty could have spawned an evil monster like Hitler?

When we finally arrive at our destination, children and instructors alike stare open-mouthed. The camp is to be held in a former convalescent home, a magnificent, several story building, overlooking a sparkling lake. We are surrounded by stunning scenery, and the fresh air is perfumed by carpets of wild flowers and woodland trees. It's an idyllic spot for a summer camp.

We are greeted by the camp supervisor, Moshe. Following a short welcome, he gives us our first task.

'The children are to be allocated bedrooms, four or

five in each room. Get them settled in, and then familiarize yourselves with the building.'

The building smells a little musty, probably due to several years of disuse, but the rooms are light and airy. We separate the boys and girls, and give them rooms on the first floor, whose only furniture are metal beds with old, but comfortable, mattresses. Then we begin our exploration.

At one end of the ground floor, next to a large kitchen, is a spacious dining hall, whose long tables can seat six to eight. The room's tall arched windows, which are partially obscured by dusty, faded drapes, offer views of the garden. At the opposite end of the building is a large room with a piano in one corner, no doubt the former patients' recreational area, for leisure activities or receiving visitors. Another room appears to have served as a classroom for recuperating children. There are desks and chairs, and a large blackboard on one wall.

On each floor there are several bathrooms, uniformly tiled in pale green ceramics bordered in black, many with free-standing, claw-footed bathtubs. The water coughs and splutters when we open the taps, and the initial flow from the rusty pipes is colored orange. In the basement, we discover several defunct treatment rooms, and what was, most probably, the laundry.

I and my fellow volunteers are given small single rooms on the top floor. Several of them complain, but I'm delighted as I survey the tiny space. The bed is wedged under the eaves, beneath a small skylight window; there is a narrow table and a chair, but not much room for anything else. I even find a ceramic chamber pot under the bed, and a pretty jug and bowl. I suppose the former staff had limited access to the bathrooms, but fortunately we are free to use the facilities whenever we like.

I imagine myself a character in one of Erna's historical romances; a maidservant, perhaps, or a governess; or a captive damsel awaiting heroic rescue. My only regret is that I don't have a view over the surrounding landscape. Never mind, there will be plenty of time to appreciate it when I'm outside with the children.

I'm not sure how I pictured everyday life in the camp, but any expectations I might have had evaporate as the first day begins. Far from being a vacation, the work is grueling. Many, if not all, of the children are sick. There are cases of tuberculosis, epilepsy, and other serious illnesses.

Much to my disgust our first unpleasant job is to delouse them. They are crawling with lice, and I shudder as I recall my train journey to captivity, and how I hacked off my infested braids. Once the children are clean, we collect and burn the rags in which most of them are dressed, and sort through boxes of clothes provided by UNRRA, trying to find something suitable for each child.

One thing all the children have in common is fear and lack of trust, which makes working with them very challenging. We take it in turns to sit up all night beside those whom sleep eludes, and to calm the ones tormented by nightmares.

It's a twenty-four hour job. The days are long and harrowing. Although I resist at first, eventually I join my colleagues in taking stimulants to help me stay awake at night.

One evening after our charges are settled in their beds, we suddenly hear screams and hysterical shouting. It seems that one of the older children has spread a rumor that the moon is about to fall out of the sky, triggering the end of the world. Of course, they believe him and pandemonium erupts. It's a clear night, so we gather the children together outside to see the brightly shining full moon.

'You see,' we assure them, 'the rumor is nonsense. The moon is watching over us and keeping us safe.'

Gradually the panic subsides. We bring out blankets and put the children to sleep on the grass, under the watchful eye of their lunar 'protector'.

Each time we think things are under control, another challenging incident sets us back. A young boy contracts a dangerous infection, and has to be quarantined to prevent an epidemic. This sparks another panic. Since no one is allowed to visit him, and he's not allowed to leave his room, the other children believe he has been taken away for some horrific medical experiment, or that he has died. Until he recovers and is reinstated with the others, we can't convince them otherwise.

Another boy falls and breaks his leg, and the local physician insists that he goes to hospital to have it set. The boy is terrified and refuses to go to a hospital.

'The Germans will take their revenge and kill me there,' he cries.

He suffers painfully for several days, until we manage to find another physician who agrees to set his leg on site.

Slowly, the children begin to relax, and the atmosphere becomes much calmer. We are able to introduce lessons into the daily routine. In the afternoons, we take them on short walks, or play games with them and, once again, I find myself in the role of story-teller, sharing the least frightening fairy tales with them, as I did with my brothers in the past. They are fascinated by the story of Ellie Smith and the Wizard of Oz. Siberia and Mikhail now seem like another lifetime.

Chapter 22

The One

Life in the summer camp is busy and challenging, and, as a result, a strong bond and feeling of camaraderie has been forged between the volunteers. Working as a team is essential for the success of our mission. There is a fairly equal ration of boys to girls, and several romantic couples evolve over the first few weeks. Most of the boys are younger than me, and I have not encouraged any of their advances. I'm nearer in age to our supervisor, Moshe, and his direct superior, Aaron. Aaron is responsible for the both the religious and secular camps, and he divides his time between the two, turning up sporadically to check on how we are doing.

Now that the children are more relaxed and trusting, we are managing to stick to a daily routine. By early evening the children are in bed, which means that we have some time to ourselves.

I am spending much of my free time with Moshe, who is easy-going and comfortable to be with. He generously offers to teach me Hebrew songs, and help me improve my vocabulary. At my request, he is also helping me with the religious content of my teaching in the camp and, more importantly, with my own personal Jewish education.

I am fascinated by his description of his life in Eretz Israel on a cooperative farm, and of the country in general. It all sounds very romantic and exotic. I picture fragrant orange groves and camels, sandy beaches and bright blue sea.

Aaron still has his car, and, now and again, the three of us manage to steal a few hours for a rare jaunt out into the countryside. I notice that Aaron usually has a camera with him, and I tell him about the loss of my treasured Leica. Kindly, he lets me take a few photos, which he brings me, after he has had the film developed.

Sitting by the lake one afternoon, Aaron asks me about my experiences during the war. I watch a range of changing emotions cross his face, as I describe the journeys, the hardships, the losses, but also the gains, of the past few years. When I finish, I'm almost as astonished as he is that I managed to survive.

'What's your story, Aaron?'

He tells me that he grew up in Breslau and that his family fled Germany in 1938, immediately after *Kristallnacht*, the Night of the Broken Glass.

Registering my puzzled expression, Aaron elaborates.

'On November 9, 1938, the Nazis initiated and carried out a pogrom against Jewish businesses and institutions across the Reich. My family lived in a smart apartment building on one of Breslau's main thoroughfares, not far from the Oder River which surrounds the city.

Late that afternoon, we were disturbed by the raucous singing and laughing of a mob of troublemakers. They were waving Nazi flags and hurling threats and insults as they headed in the direction of our synagogue, which was set back from the road behind an archway in a secluded courtyard. Soon we heard the sound of shattered glass.

Instructing my mother and younger brother and sister to stay indoors and out of sight, my father took me and my older brother to see what was happening. Horrified, we watched as the invaders pillaged the synagogue, throwing Torah scrolls and prayer books out of the smashed windows into the courtyard, where others trampled, ripped, and spat upon them, before torching them and the building.

My brother and I tried to put out the flames and rescue some of the precious treasure, but the hoodlums violently pushed us away. We retreated with burned fingers, blackened faces and singed hair, clutching just one single piece of scorched parchment, which we took with us to Eretz Israel.'

Aaron describes in painful detail the scene that greeted Breslau's Jews the following morning. Jewish shops, apartment buildings, schools and businesses bore the devastating evidence of the Night of the Broken Glass; vandalized books and property, smashed doorways and piles of shards from broken windows.

'This was the final warning signal for my father. Until then, he had thought that our family was not in danger. After all, his older brother Ernst, of blessed memory, had been a highly esteemed officer in the German army, decorated with the Iron Cross for bravery in the First World War.'

Aaron explains that the family owned a large fish import and marketing business which supplied fish to the German army, and that his father was on good terms with government officials. But after witnessing Kristallnacht, he understood this was no longer a guarantee of safety, and that he had to get the family out of Germany.

'Luckily, father had connections to several shipping companies. One of the owners with whom he was friendly agreed to smuggle us out on one of his ships. We were lucky to escape when we did.'

When Aaron finishes telling his story, I amaze him by recounting my visit to his hometown, and my unsuccessful attempt to enroll in the university there.

'Breslau has been renamed Wroclaw. The city has suffered badly and I saw large-scale destruction there.'

'What about the Market Square and Centennial Hall? I remember them clearly from my childhood.'

'They are still intact; and so is anti-Semitism, just as it was before the war,' I tell him.

'Jews will never be accepted there, or have an opportunity to reclaim their possessions.'

The summer program lasts for two months. When it ends, the children, much healthier and in far better spirits, are returned to the camps they came from. The counsellors, however, remain for an instruction seminar, and finally, we get our chance to rest and relax.

The counsellors from the other camp join us, as well as more emissaries from Eretz Israel. Moshe and I spend lazy days, discussing the past and the future, taking long walks, and boating on the lake. It's so reminiscent of carefree summer afternoons before the war in Tsanz's *Venice* park.

On the last night before we all head our separate ways, I lay in bed wondering what my next step should be. Aaron has suggested that I return to Steyr, to my family, and he's offered me a teaching position in the school. It seems that he's responsible for all the schools in displaced persons camps in Austria.

Before taking charge of the summer camp program he was based in the town of Linz, but he has taken on additional work with the *Bricha* movement, so he plans to make his base in Steyr, which is nearer the border. I decide to confer with Moshe.

'Take the job, Tanya,' he advises me.

'When you get to Eretz Israel your teaching experience will be invaluable.'

Mama and Papa are thrilled to see me return. And a delighted

Mr. Klingman wastes no time in introducing his new teacher to the rest of his staff. Unlike summer camp, the school day has regular hours, and my responsibilities are limited to teaching. As before, there are children of varying ages and abilities, who speak different languages - Polish, Russian Hungarian, Yiddish, German - but lessons are taught in Hebrew, which is to become their common tongue.

Thrown in at the deep end once again, I discover that in my class I have two deaf and dumb children, and I have to find special ways to reach them. Each crumb of success with them gives me a marvelous feeling of satisfaction and achievement. Because of the shortage of educators, I am also required to teach my students a wide variety of subjects – geography, nature, math, and even good manners – how to eat politely, how to address their elders, to say *please* and *thank you*.

More than anything else, I am bombarded with their questions. So many questions, about so many things. Everything is new to them. They are thirsty for answers, for knowledge, and I'm happy to share what little I have. I also tell them about the Promised Land of Eretz Israel, repeating stories I have heard from Moshe and other emissaries.

Life in the camp is not all work, however. Quite a lively social scene has developed. There's an amateur theater group, which puts on Yiddish plays, and even a small orchestra. Every so often, a touring musical troupe provides us with an evening's entertainment. Whenever there is dancing, I'm the first to join in, not only with the traditional *hora*, but also with some of the Bukharan steps I learned in Tajikistan, which I adapt to the Klezmer music.

'Just like a wild gypsy,' Mama grumbles, embarrassed by my exhibitionism.

Perhaps these are the good times predicted for me by the kindly Romany woman in Khodoriv. I worry about what fate might have befallen her. The Nazis also murdered gypsies.

Mama is also annoyed that I have not responded more positively to the romantic overtures that have been made towards me by several young men. They are all very personable, and I have agreed to spend time with one or two of them, but there is no spark, no weak-at-the-knees attraction.

'You're not getting any younger, Tanya,' Mama reminds me over and over.

'Look at all these other girls getting married. Soon there'll be no one left for you.'

I would rather remain a spinster than marry someone I don't love, and I don't intend to let Mama's pressure influence me. Papa, as usual, is supportive, even though I'm sure he would like to see me happily settled.

Aaron lives in Steyr but spends much of his time elsewhere, carrying out his numerous duties. Whenever he can, he pops by school to find out how I'm getting on, and seems to take a genuine interest in my progress. He's older and much more mature than the other young men I'm friendly with, and I enjoy his company and our conversations, especially since Moshe is occupied elsewhere. Unfortunately, I find his smoking habit very distasteful.

Whenever he leaves camp late at night, I know he is on his way to take part in Bricha operations, driving trucks of escapees from Czechoslovakia and Hungary, and distributing them among the camps in the area. Having been on missions myself, I'm well aware of the risks, and I worry for his safety.

One evening, Mr. Klingman comes to see me.

'Tanya, I know you have become quite friendly with Aaron. I thought you should know that he was on a special mission in Prague, where he was caught taking photographs. The Russians have arrested him for spying.'

'Thank you for letting know,' I reply, hardly able to put the words together.

I can't catch my breath, and my heart is pounding, fear coursing through my veins at the very thought of what Klingman has told me. I grab on to a chair for support. I picture Aaron driving us to a picnic in the country, taking photos of me with his camera, chatting about his childhood in Germany and his life in Eretz Israel, encouraging me to teach. And in that instant, I realize something I have been stubbornly denying to myself for months. Aaron is *The One*. The one I have been waiting for.

I recognize now that my feelings for Mikhail were just a schoolgirl crush, a desperate escape into romanticism from my miserable existence. My feelings for Aaron go much, much deeper, down to the core of my being. He is my soulmate.

I go over in my mind our recent meetings and conversations, and it's clear that Aaron's interest in me is not just professional curiosity. He has been giving me hints that I have stupidly chosen to ignore. And now I don't know what I'll do if he doesn't return safely.

Several days pass in a blur. Papa is concerned by my behavior.

'Tanya'leh, what's the matter? You don't seem like yourself.'

I tell him about Aaron's arrest, and confess my feelings for him.

'Well, even if you couldn't see it, it's obvious to everyone else that you two are made for each other. Aaron won't abandon you that easily. I'm sure he'll find a way to get back soon.'

A few more nerve-wracking days go by, and still there's no news. I carry out my teaching duties as best I can, thankful that my responsibilities to the children give me a focus, and help me pass the hours. But the evenings are long and lonely, allowing my imagination to conjure up gruesome mental pictures of Aaron in a Russian prison.

But, as always, Papa is right. By some miracle, Aaron is released, and a week later he returns to Steyr. As soon as I hear familiar footfalls in the corridor outside my room, I run to open my door and throw myself into his arms, my heart beating wildly as I tremble with relief and desire at the sight of him.

'Tanya, I have something of the greatest importance to ask you.'

'Yes, I will,' I interrupt, before he has the chance to complete his marriage proposal.

Folding me into his warm embrace, Aaron seals our engagement with a kiss that seems to last forever, more intense and passionate than anything written in a silly romantic novel.

Chapter 23

Homeward Bound, 1948

Excitement in Steyr has been building since last November, when the United Nations General Assembly passed a resolution, calling for Palestine to be partitioned between Arabs and Jews, and allowing for the formation of the Jewish State of Israel. I have spent many hours with my students making flags and banners, streamers and confetti, in anticipation of the Declaration of Independence. Finally, on May fourteenth, the day the British mandate in Palestine comes to an end, we hear David Ben-Gurion's words over the radio:

'*It is the self-evident right of the Jewish people to be a nation, as all other nations, in their own sovereign state. By virtue of the natural and historic right of the Jewish people and of the Resolution of the General Assembly of the United Nations, we hereby proclaim the establishment of the Jewish State in Palestine to be called Israel.*'

The level of rejoicing is exhilarating. Everyone is kissing and hugging, and then come tears of joy and relief, and prayers of thanksgiving, acknowledging God's mercy in allowing us to survive, and to witness this miraculous day. And of course, more tears for those who didn't survive.

Children and adults spontaneously form circles and dance the *hora*, the traditional Jewish celebration dance. Flags are waving, streamers are billowing, and confetti is catching in people's hair. A band is playing song after song, *Hava Nagila (Let us rejoice), Siman Tov u'Mazal Tov (A good sign and good luck), David Melech Israel (David King of Israel)*, and we dance round and round, until we are dizzy and breathless. And as the celebration winds down, we stand to attention and reverently sing the words of *Hatikvah*, The Hope, our national anthem.

> *'As long as the Jewish spirit is yearning deep in the heart,*
> *With eyes turned toward the East, looking toward Zion,*
> *Then our hope - the two-thousand-year-old hope - will not be lost:*
> *To be a free people in our land,*
> *The land of Zion and Jerusalem.'*

The rejoicing is short-lived, however, as war erupts as soon as the declaration is made, and the newborn state is attacked by Arab armies on all sides. A recruitment office is set up in the camp and all eligible young men are conscripted. My brother Jozef goes behind Mama's and Papa's backs and signs up, even though he's underage. He's not quite seventeen, but passes himself off as eighteen. The desperate need for soldiers is so great that he is accepted without too many questions being asked.

'Tanya,' he informs me, proudly. 'I'm leaving tomorrow with the next group. We'll receive some basic training in Italy, and then we're off to defend our homeland.'

I hug him to me, hardly able to believe that this is the same boy who was frightened by my ghoulish fairy tales not so many years ago. Mama and Papa are furious, but it's too late to stop him. Despite their justified worries, they wave him off, tearful but proud of his patriotism and courage.

Aaron also wants to enlist, but his superiors refuse to let him to go, saying that his job here is more important. He has also received a letter from his father in Jerusalem, advising him to stay in Austria, saying *'Your brother has enlisted. He will fight for the two of you.'* We've discussed this at length, and it's difficult for me to watch his inner turmoil and indecision.

Finally, one evening he comes to my room.

'Tanya, I can't stay here while others are risking their lives.

My patriotic duty must come before my emissary work. I have decided to go home.'

Since this comes as no surprise, I'm prepared for his half-expected decision.

'If you go, so do I. I've made inquiries, and it seems they are accepting women into special units of new immigrants conscripted overseas. I'll sign up and we'll leave together.'

A few days later, Aaron and I find ourselves traveling with a large group of volunteers to Marseille, in the South of France, and from there, by ship to Israel.

After hearing of the harrowing experiences of the *Exodus*, and other ships of all shapes and sizes that tried to outwit the British in order to bring Jewish refugees to the shores of Eretz Israel, we feel elated and triumphant as our ship, displaying its blue and white flag, steams legally into Haifa port. No more clandestine illegal immigration, no more British blockade, no more turning back.

The deck is packed, and all the passengers jostle each other and crane their necks to get a first glimpse of their new homeland. Tears flow as we spontaneously join together in one voice to sing *Hatikvah*, and wave wildly to the well-wishers waiting on the wharf to welcome the new arrivals.

The ship docks and I disembark. My odyssey of almost ten years has been long and tortuous, traversing thousands of kilometers from West to East, North to South, and East to West. Finally, I have reached home.

Sadly, Aaron and I only have a few minutes together to savor the moment before we are whisked off in different directions, each one to an appointed destination.

I am sent to work in army headquarters in Jaffa. Much to my dismay, when I arrive I discover that I'm to work in the office which receives news of casualties. It's my job to collect the names of the fallen soldiers, and pass them on to those responsible for notifying their families.

Aaron has joined his army unit in the Givati Brigade on the southern front, which is defending the country from the advancing Egyptian army in the Negev desert. Fighting is fierce and casualties are high. Every day a new list of the unlucky ones arrives on my desk, and my heart races as I scan the names, praying that Aaron's will not be among them.

I also fear for my brother Jozef. The family has had no communication from him, and I have no idea where he is.

One morning, as I look down the list of names, I receive a nasty jolt. Tears spring to my eyes as I recognize a familiar name. It belongs to one of the boys who learned to milk cows with me on the kibbutz in Germany. He was the last surviving member of his entire family. And now he, too, is gone.

On a brighter note, Mama and Papa have arrived in Israel. They have been reunited with a number of family members who survived the war, including Mama's brother, the uncle who Daniel helped me find. One of Papa's aunts has kindly given me a room in her apartment in Tel Aviv, which is convenient for work.

Tel Aviv surprises me. Expecting the sand and camels I imagined from Moshe's stories, I'm amazed to find a bustling, modern metropolis and commercial center, with hotels, theaters and cinemas. In my free time, I wander the streets, admiring the unique *Bauhaus* buildings, designed by German Jewish architects who fled the Nazis and immigrated to the British Mandate of Palestine in the 1930s; on Rothschild Boulevard, where Israel's independence was declared; on Hayarkon Street, near the beach; on Bialik Street, named for the national poet.

The Dizengoff circle is a little oasis in the center of town, offering benches on manicured grass verges under palm trees, where it's pleasantly refreshing to sit and watch the performance of a large fountain in the middle. From there, I enjoy strolling along Dizengoff Street, which is lined with stores and fashionable coffee houses. Some days it's even possible to forget that war is raging just a few kilometers away.

I feel guilty that, despite the gruesome nature of my work, and the profound sadness I feel for the families of those poor men and boys who appear daily on my lists, I'm taking such pleasure in my new surroundings, and in acclimatizing myself to my new life.

From time to time, there are lulls in the fighting and Aaron manages a brief visit, but all too soon he has to return to his unit. He doesn't tell me much about his experiences, but he has lost some weight, and fatigue is etched on his face. I worry about him constantly.

Five months after we land in Israel, I receive a note from Aaron telling me to expect a visit the following day. From hushed whispers in the corridors in my office building I have learned that Egyptian forces have advanced to positions a mere thirty-five kilometers to the south of Tel Aviv. In my job I'm privy, officially and unofficially, to some information before it is made public, and I'm terrified that Aaron is coming to say 'Goodbye' to me before he sets out on a particularly dangerous mission. But he reassures me, saying that he has a surprise for me. I can't imagine what it could be, but surprises are generally good, so I'm excited to find out what it is.

When he arrives he wastes no time in getting to the point.

'Look, Tanya. It's war time. No one knows what tomorrow may bring. I want us to get married right away. Your parents are here, my parents are here, what are we waiting for?'

Of course, he gets no argument from me.

The whirlwind wedding is arranged in no time at all. Mama tracks down a cousin whose daughter recently got married, and borrows the wedding dress, which she alters to fit me. Aaron's father is acquainted with Rabbi Frenkel, the Chief Rabbi of Tel Aviv, and Papa is honored that he not only agrees to conduct the ceremony, but also offers his own apartment for the occasion. Resources are very limited, so my aunt and Mama, helped by a couple of other female relatives, cater the refreshments themselves. Aaron is granted a week's leave and the date is set. I'm also allowed to take a week off work.

However, a couple of weeks before the appointed day, an Israeli supply convoy, under United Nations supervision, sets out on its way to besieged towns and villages in the Negev through enemy lines, and is fired upon by the Egyptian forces. In retaliation, our army launches an offensive operation, and it seems that the Givati Brigade has been charged with knocking out the deadly Egyptian stronghold positions, in order to clear a safe corridor to the south.

My taut nerves are stretched to snapping point, as notifications of more and more casualties darken my desk, including names of comrades mentioned to me by Aaron in the past weeks. I feel like I've been holding my breath for days, when I finally hear from Aaron that he is safe, and I can allow myself to exhale, and release some of the overwhelming tension.

At last, our special day arrives, and the very small wedding party gathers in the rabbi's apartment at two in the afternoon, late enough to give Aaron sufficient time to get to Tel Aviv from where he's stationed. Time passes, but no Aaron. As the clock ticks by, I begin to get anxious. The rabbi doesn't have a phone, and anyway I wouldn't know who to contact.

Papa takes my hand. 'Don't worry, Tanya'leh, he'll be here.' Another tense hour passes, and still no word. Suddenly there's a knock at the door. I look nervously at Papa, and we watch with bated breath as the rabbi goes to open it. Aaron rushes in, looking unkempt and flustered, and apologizes for the delay.

He explains that the driver of his jeep took a wrong turn, and they found themselves in unfamiliar, hostile territory. In order to get out safely they had to take a lengthy, convoluted route, through desert terrain.

'Hence the dust,' Aaron concludes, looking mortified and brushing himself off.

I realize too late that no one thought to engage a photographer to record the happy day. In the event, it's probably just as well. The bride, in her hand-me-down, not too flattering dress, and the disheveled groom in his grimy uniform, wouldn't make a very memorable picture.

The guest list numbers a little over single figures, and despite my happiness, I mourn silently for those who can't be with us; for my darling Erna; for my beloved Grandfather, and Little Bubbe, and Papa's brother Herschel; for Mr. Samuels and his two horses; for Magda and her family; for friends who did not survive the rigors of Siberia. And when, under the wedding canopy, it's time for Aaron to give the blessing of thanksgiving, I take his hand and recite it together with him. '*Barukh ata adonai elohenu melekh ha'olam, shehecheyanu, v'kiyimanu, v'higiyanu la'z'man ha'zeh.*' Blessed are You Lord our God, Ruler of the Universe, who has given us life, sustained us, and allowed us to reach this day.

Chapter 24

Home, 1949

'Where are we going to live?' I whisper to Aaron after the ceremony.

Papa's *three esses* come back to haunt me. Obviously, we can't move in with my aunt or any other relatives. We have very little money, and accommodation is scarce. We spend the first two days of our 'honeymoon' looking for somewhere to live, and eventually come across a small room in a building on the edge of Tel Aviv, where it borders on Jaffa, which we can just about afford.

In reality, it's a room within a room. In order to get to it we have to pass through a room belonging to another family. The shared kitchen and lavatory are in the yard. Memories of Siberia come flooding back. But now times are different, and I can look back almost laughingly. We have a room to ourselves and we're happy, and that's all that matters. We manage to buy a cupboard, and, most importantly, a proper bed, where my fantasies are finally, and joyfully, fulfilled. It's inconvenient that every time we want to go out of our room we have to knock on the door and ask our neighbors if it's alright to go through. But it's fine, and no one complains. After all, there are people in far worse conditions than ours.

The honeymoon ends only too quickly, and Aaron has to return to his unit. When I go back to work, I'm annoyed to discover that I have been transferred to a different department.

My new job entails completing paperwork reporting military traffic accidents. What happened, where it happened, and how it happened. The work is excruciatingly boring, but at least it takes my mind off worrying about Aaron.

Hostilities continue for another five months, and then, finally, the war is over. It's time to decide what our next move will be. Aaron told me back in Steyr that he intended to return to his studies. At the first opportunity, he applies, and is accepted, for study at the Hebrew University in Jerusalem. He will live my dream for me, and I am happy for both of us.

Papa promised me that one day I would study there, but now that it's possible, it's not practical. But I'm not disappointed. I'm already pregnant, and full time study is not an option. Anyway, we can't afford two students in the family. Someone has to put food on the table, and not just for the two of us. Rare are the evenings when Aaron comes home alone, without some student or other, who has no family and is in need of a home-cooked meal.

The proceeds we get from selling our room and furniture in Tel Aviv are enough for a down payment on a long-term rental in Zion Square, in the center of Jerusalem. The apartment is luxurious in comparison to our previous accommodation, with two bedrooms, a living room and kitchen, and our very own bathroom. It's on the third floor, reached by a winding staircase, which becomes increasingly challenging as my pregnancy progresses.

Times are hard in the newborn State; food is rationed, goods are hard to come by, and money is scarce. Once again, we are buying goods with vouchers and points, but we are comfortable and content, and I don't resent it, as I did in Siberia and in the DP camps. Life has purpose and a future.

Because I have a matriculation certificate from Russia, and some hands-on experience, I'm easily accepted to teacher training college. In little over a year, I'm working as a *qualified* teacher in a local school. I recall Papa's advice when we arrived in Siberia, that I should take every opportunity to learn new skills, since one day they may be useful. Luckily, I have no use for my grave-digging or milking expertise, but my experiences teaching children in the DP camps have definitely prepared me well for my new career.

Mama and Papa have also moved to Jerusalem with Dovid, and have been joined by Jozef, who was recently released from the army. As soon as they were settled, Papa, of course, established an ice-cream and candy factory across the street from their house. Mama helps to take care of my beautiful baby boy while I'm at work.

I look back on my interrupted life, and a ten year odyssey fraught with fear, deprivation and disruption, hopelessness and hopefulness, physical and psychological pain. The losses and suffering were overwhelming, but, somehow, they didn't defeat me. Thanks to Mikhail's mantra '*Anything is possible*' and Ellie Smith, I managed to find the positive in the negative, and acknowledge that good can come from evil.

I lost my home, but gained a homeland. I lost my freedom, but gained my independence. I lost much of my formal education, but discovered that there's a lot to be learned from life's lessons. My involuntary wanderings exposed me to undreamed-of experiences: the breathtaking aurora borealis; the treasures of the State Library of Leningrad; the culture of exotic central Asia. I have lost dear friends and relatives, who sadly cannot be replaced, but I have gained a soulmate, and together we are building our own new family.

Tonight we will celebrate Passover. This year there is no need for an imaginary Seder. The table is set with a white tablecloth, and the special Seder plate, displaying the six items which remind us of the Passover story. There are no crystal wine goblets or delicate porcelain dishes, but we do have real wine, produced in an Israeli vineyard, and there are plenty of matzos for all.

We will be joined by my friend Luba and her family, and several of Aaron's 'strays', as I like to call them. Dovid will ask the four questions, now old enough not to require any prompting by me, and we will enjoy Mama's chicken soup with matzo balls.

We will eat the bitter herbs, and recall not only the Israelites' exodus from Egypt, but also our own wandering, exile and slavery in Siberia.

And at the end of the evening we will all joyfully shout:

'**THIS** year in Jerusalem!'

Epilogue

Of Bitter Herbs and Sweet Confections is based on the memoirs of the author's late mother-in-law, Tamar Englander Shalev. While sitting *shiva* (seven days of mourning) for her mother in 1987, Tamar was persuaded by her daughter to record her memoirs. The tapes were put aside, and only rediscovered a few years after her death.

The historical events are accurate, and the protagonist's experiences, while fictionalized and embellished are, for the most part, true to life. Characters' names have been changed or invented as necessary.

Following the experiences described in this book, Tamar spent her entire working life in education, specializing in children with learning difficulties, such as dyslexia.

Tamar married Avraham Friedlander Shalev in November 1948. They were blessed with three children, eleven grandchildren, and, to date, twenty-five great grandchildren. Avraham passed away in 2004, and Tamar in 2008.

While Tamar's long-held dream of attending the Hebrew University in Jerusalem never came true, Avraham gained his Master's Degree from the institution, and four of their grandchildren are alumni.

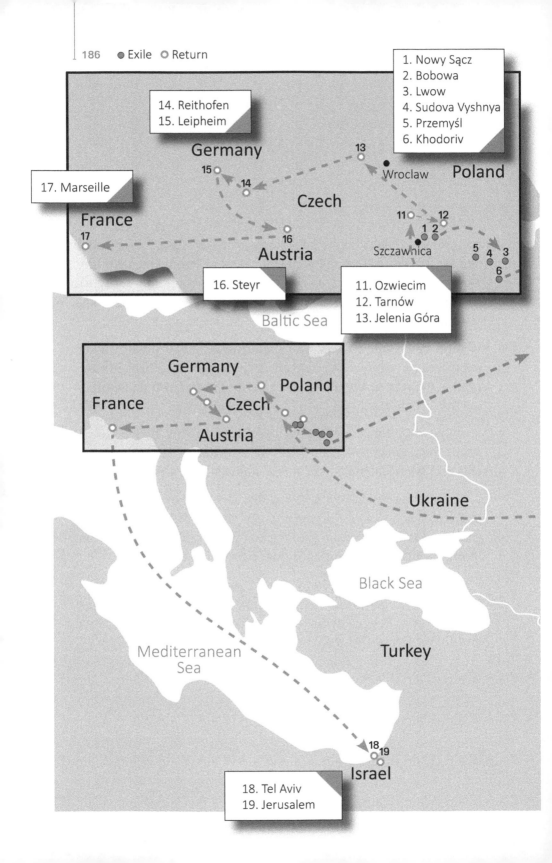

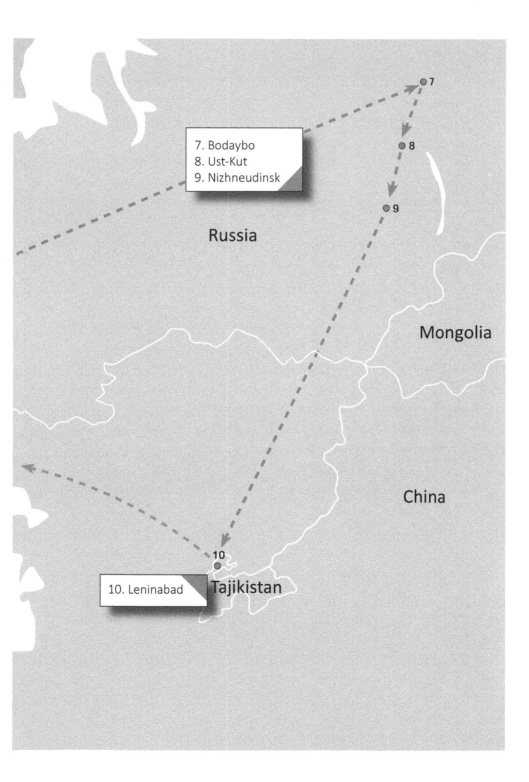

7. Bodaybo
8. Ust-Kut
9. Nizhneudinsk

Russia

Mongolia

China

10. Leninabad

Tajikistan

Author's Notes

Chapter 1:

Tajikistan is a mountainous, landlocked country in Central Asia, bordered by Afghanistan to the south, Uzbekistan to the west, Kyrgyzstan to the north, and China to the east.

Chapter 2:

Founded by the Duke of Kraków in 1292, Nowy Sącz (*Neu Sandez* in German, *Tsanz* in Yiddish) is one of the oldest cities in the Lesser Poland region. It is located twenty kilometers north of the Slovak border.

Bubbe and *Zayde* are Yiddish endearments for grandma and grandpa.

Chapter 3:

In Jewish folklore and popular belief a *dybbuk* is an evil spirit, which enters into a living person and captures his/her soul, speaking through his/her mouth, as a separate and alien personality.

Chapter 4:

Before the Holocaust, the village of Bobowa was notable as an historic center of *Hasidism*, an Orthodox spiritual revivalist movement that emerged in Eastern Europe in the 18th century. Followers of Hasidic Judaism (known as Hasidim, or "pious ones") drew heavily on the Jewish mystical tradition in seeking a direct experience of God through ecstatic prayer, and other rituals conducted under the spiritual direction of a Rebbe, a charismatic leader sometimes also known as a *tzaddik* , or righteous man. After the Second World War, Rabbi Shlomo Halberstam (1907-2000), son of the Bobowa Rebbe who perished in the Holocaust, re-established the Bobov Hassidic dynasty in America. It now has branches in New York, Montreal, Toronto, Antwerp, London and Israel.

Chapter 5:

Sudova Vyshnya is located about fifty kilometers west of Lwow, and three hundred kilometers from Nowy Sącz. During the September 1939 invasion of Poland, the Battle of Jaworów took place in the area near the town. German armed forces stationed in the town included an elite unit of SS Galicia. Only three of the town's Jews survived the war.

Chapter 6:

In Operation Barbarossa of 1941, the eastern (Soviet) part of Przemyśl was re-occupied by Germany. On 20 June, 1942, the first group of 1,000 Jews was transported to the Janowska concentration camp, and on 15 July, 1942, a ghetto was established for all Jewish inhabitants of Przemyśl and its vicinity – some 22,000 people altogether. By September 1943, almost all Jews had been sent to the Auschwitz or Belzec extermination camps.

Chapter 7:

Khodoriv, also known as Chodorów, is 380 kilometers from Nowy Sącz, in the Lwow district. Built in the mid-17th century, the Chodorów synagogue was famous for its beauty. The Jewish 'Michelangelo' who painted the ceiling, was Israel Ben Mordechai Lissnicki, an itinerant artist. A beautifully reconstructed full-color model of the Chodorów ceiling can be seen in the Museum of the Jewish People (Bet Hatfutsot) in Tel Aviv. In September and October 1942, the Nazis, having taken the town from the Russians, deported the Jews from Khodoriv to the extermination camp in Belzec. The synagogue was destroyed.

Chapter 9:

Bodaybo on the Vitim River, some 7,600 kilometers from Nowy Sącz, is located 1,500 kilometers from Irkutsk, one of Siberia's major cities located on Lake Baikal near the Mongolian border.

Chapter 10:

Tanya's father suffered from Xerophthalmia, or night blindness, due to Vitamin A deficiency.

Chapter 11:

Tanya's romantic interlude with Mikhail is a figment of the author's imagination. There was, indeed, a benevolent teacher who encouraged the students and gave them hope. Someone, most likely the Tatar teacher, reported him to the authorities for fraternizing with prisoners, and he was arrested and taken away to stand trial.

Chapter 12:

The festival of Passover falls in spring. During the reading of the *Haggadah*, the book which tells the story of the Israelites' exodus from Egypt, it is customary for the youngest participant to ask four questions in the text, the answers to which explain the traditions of the festive *Seder* meal.

Chapter 13:

In the early 20th century, Ust-Kut on the Lena River served as a destination for political exiles, most notably Leon Trotsky.

The German Siege of Leningrad claimed 650,000 lives in 1942 alone, mostly from starvation, exposure, disease, and shelling from distant German artillery.

Chapter 14:
The All-Union Leninist Young Communist League, usually known as Komsomol, a syllabic abbreviation of the Russian *kommunisticheskiy soyuz molodyozhi*, was a political youth organization in the Soviet Union, sometimes described as the youth division of the Communist Party, although it was officially independent. Every aspect of a Komsomolets's life was to be in accordance with Party doctrine. Smoking, drinking, religion, and any other activity the Bolsheviks saw as threatening, were discouraged as "hooliganism".

Chapter 15:
Leninabad is the former name of Khujand. Khujand is one of the oldest cities in Central Asia, dating back about 2,500 years. It is 5,000 kilometers from Nowy Sącz. The city was renamed Leninabad in 1936, and it remained part of the Soviet Union until 1991. With the independence of Tajikistan, Khujand became the second largest city in the nation. It reverted to its original name in 1992.

Chapter 16:
The SS authorities established three main camps near the Polish city of Oswiecim. It is estimated that between 1940 and 1945, 1,095,000 Jews were deported to the Auschwitz complex, of whom 960,000 died; 147,000 Poles, of whom 74,000 died; 23,000 Roma, of whom 21,000 died; 15,000 Soviet prisoners of war, none of whom survived; and 25,000 other nationalities, of whom 12,000 died.

Before World War II, about 25,000 Jews lived in Tarnów, comprising almost half of the town's total population. Deportations from Tarnów began in June 1942, when about 13,500 Jews were sent to the Belzec extermination camp. From 11–19 June, 1942, the Germans gathered thousands of Jews in the Rynek (market place), where they were tortured and killed.

During this time period, on the streets of the town and in the Jewish cemetery, about 3,000 Jews were shot. After the June deportations, the Germans forced the surviving Jews of Tarnów, along with thousands of Jews from neighboring towns, into the new Tarnów Ghetto. The Germans decided to destroy the Tarnów ghetto in September 1943. The surviving 10,000 Jews were deported to Auschwitz and to the Plaszow concentration camp in Kraków. In late 1943, Tarnów was declared "free of Jews" (*Judenrein*).

Chapter 17:

During the Nazi regime, universities regularly stripped degrees and titles from Jews, and other scholars seen as hostile to the Nazis, and the then University of Breslau stood at the forefront of this dubious practice. In January 2015, the now University of Wroclaw restored 262 PhD degrees withdrawn during the Nazi period.

The Nowy Sącz Ghetto, Ghetto von Neu-Sandez in German, incarcerating around 20,000 Jewish people from the city and neighboring villages, was established by the German authorities near the castle. Its inhabitants were deported to Belzec extermination camp over three days in August 1942. The Red Army fought its way into the city on 20 January, 1945. At war's end, about 60% of the city had been destroyed. Before the war, nearly a third of the city's population was Jewish; ninety percent of them died or did not return.

Chapter 18:

Many Zionist youth movements were established in Eastern Europe in the early twentieth century. Their goal was the national revival of the Jewish people in their own homeland, and they were an active and integral part of the Zionist movement. They played a considerable role in politics, Jewish education, and community organization, particularly between the two world wars. Their members were the nucleus of the Jewish resistance movements in the ghettos and camps of the Holocaust, and of the partisans. They also led the escape (*Bricha*) movement from Europe following the war.

Chapter 19:

Pinchas Burstein (1927–1977) was a Polish-born Jewish post-expressionist painter. Born in Nowy Sącz, he was sent, aged twelve, to the Auschwitz concentration camp, where he lost his leg. After the war, he spent the years 1945–1947 in Germany, in the camps for displaced persons, and from 1947 to 1950, he lived in Israel, where he studied in the Bezalel Academy of Art and Design in Jerusalem. In 1950, Burstein arrived in Paris, where he studied at the Ecole Nationale Superieure des Beaux-Arts. He produced largely autobiographical work, holding major exhibitions in Jerusalem and Paris. Moving to New York in 1962, he changed his name to Maryan S. Maryan. He committed suicide in 1977, and is buried in the Montparnasse cemetery in Paris.

Chapter 21:

Aaron's real name is Avraham Friedlander (changed to Shalev in 1951).

Chapter 23:

Exodus 1947 was a ship that carried 4,500 Jewish immigrants from France to British Mandatory Palestine on July 11, 1947. Most were Holocaust survivors, who had no legal immigration certificates. The ship was attacked by the British in international waters, killing four passengers and wounding over one hundred. The ship was taken to Haifa, where prison ships were waiting to return the Jews to refugee camps in Europe.

Chapter 24:

The Hebrew University was founded in 1918, and opened in 1925. Today, it is ranked internationally among the 100 leading universities in the world, and first among Israeli universities. To date it has produced eight Nobel Prize winners.

Acknowledgments

I am deeply grateful to my sister-in-law, Ziva Shalev Maskowitz, for encouraging her mother to tell her story, on which this book is based; to my brother-in-law, Dr. Itzhak Shalev, for his editing of the original Hebrew transcript and preliminary background research; and to my husband, Uri, and my family and friends for their invaluable input and support.

About the Author

Susan Shalev was born and raised in London, England. She immigrated to Israel in 1976, and married her husband Uri in the same year. The couple has four children and nine grandchildren. She holds a BA Honors degree in Psychology from Manchester University, UK, an MSc in Industrial Relations from Strathclyde University, UK, and in 2016 she was awarded a PhD in Sociology and Anthropology from Bar-Ilan University, Israel.

Of Bitter Herbs and Sweet Confections is the author's literary debut.

Thank you for reading *Of Bitter Herbs and Sweet Confections*. **If you have enjoyed it please consider leaving a short review on Amazon or wherever you can.**